Adventures
of
Aros

For
Aros and
its Queen,
the family,
Ralph
and his loved ones.

♥
special thanks to:
Rashard Williams
for helping with the
translation!

written:
Florian H. Azar

Introduction to role play
Character sheet explanation
Create heroes
Game master
Dice samples
Experience points
Combat system
Develop story

The world of Aros

Catch and train monsters
Monster
places
Plants & Mushrooms

Playing with game board

Game sheets for free
on
www.azar-games.de

Introduction to Roleplaying Games

The Kingdom of Aros is an easy to learn fantasy game for casual gamers and children aged 6+. The world of Aros is shaped by myths, magic, powerful warriors, fantastic beasts and monsters. In a time without electricity, computers and smartphones, a group of heroes must embark on adventures, defeat monsters and bosses, protect the innocent and recover treasures. Aros can only be played with pen, paper and dice. Aros can also be played with a game board and figures. All battles are then fought out based on a tactical board game.

Welcome to Aros

Merkand had to blink. The sun blazed straight into his face through the dense foliage. The scent of fresh forest soil, moss, and mushrooms slowly woke him up. He loved sleeping in the woods. There was something very soothing about all those smells and sounds. He sat up and his eyes wandered searchingly to his comrades. Mirna, a pale, slightly bluish Elf, seemed to be still asleep. Her cold white hair contrasted beautifully with the rich green of the moss she was lying on. She clutched her bow tightly.

Further to the right lay Kant, the dwarf. A burly fellow. Not particularly tall, but wide and strong. Kant was a small, tough fighting machine. He didn't even take off his handsome armor to sleep. How could you sleep in a thing like that? Merkand couldn't imagine it. Trying was out of the question for him. He enjoyed too much sleeping on the warm and soft forest floor. Suddenly...something worried him.

His gaze wandered to Agorna. The thief lay stretched out on the ground. Her hands clasped on her chest, clutching both of her throwing knives. She looked tense. Maybe she had a bad dream. Maybe the ghosts from her past came back in her dreams. The unsettling feeling that something was wrong here grew. What's wrong here, Merkand thought. Everything looked the same as always, but something was missing. A detail, a triviality, was not in its place. His wand lay beside him on the soft ground. His hand slowly moves towards it and he grasps the old staff in one hand. His movements were slow and quiet.

The strange feeling increased. His nose and mind reacted almost simultaneously. Kant doesn't snore. Kant always snores. Kant usually snores so loudly that it can be heard far beyond the forest. At the same moment, he noticed the slightly musty smell. He recognized the smell and immediately knew where it came from. Puddle henrys! Those slimy beasts looked like puddles. They flowed over the ground like water and can only be identified by their musty smell. If you weren't careful, they'd fall upon you, and the poisonous ooze from their stomachs would digest you to the bone.

Merkand glanced at Mirna. Her eyes were slightly open. She winked at Merkand. As she jumped up, drew her bow, and screamed. Kant jumped up and brandished his mighty war hammer. Agorna did the same. In a feline move, she jumped to her feet. In each hand, she held a throwing knife. Merkand was the last of the. He jumped up and raised his staff and shouted "Blood Heaven of Kernach". A red bolt of lightning struck in front of him. A puddle in front of him rose into a massive slime monster. The heat of the lightning had burned a huge hole in his body. The evaporating liquid formed clouds of fog. He yelled, "Leave no one alive!"

Introduction to role play

Kingdom of Aros is a classic role-playing game. In a role-playing game, one player takes on the role of the narrator (master) and several players take on the role of heroes. The master guides this group of heroes through a prepared adventure with his tales. Each hero has a herosheet on which all skills, weapons, and other items are listed. Heroes have different valueslike attack, defense, intelligence, strength, dexterity, etc. Battles and skill checks are determined by rolling dice. How much damage an attack causes, or whether a lock can be picked thanks to dexterity, depends on the dice roll.

Heroes can improve and upgrade their skills as the game progresses. In this way, tasks can be mastered more easily in the future, and the level of difficulty of the tasks can increase steadily. Since each hero has individual skills, it makes sense to use them profitably for the group. Someone who has a high level of dexteritiy, for example, is better at picking locks. Those with higher intelligence can, for example, speak different languages and those with more charisma will find it easier to influence other people.

hero sheet

The hero sheet describes the hero and his abilities. What is the name of our hero? What race and class does he belong to. How many life points does he have. Which weapon does the hero use and which skills characterize him. In the notes section, heroes can note special items. The hero's maximum life points can be noted in the heart symbol.

The top of the hero sheet shows 4 symbols. These symbols represent different attributes. These attributes are used for combat, defense, movement, and weapon range. If Aros is played with figures and a board, these 4 attributes are crucial for tactical combat. More about playing with a gameboard in a later chapter.

All skills can be improved and expanded. For this purpose, there are circles behind the corresponding skills. The better a hero is in an area, the more circles he can tick or color on the hero sheet. Skills can vary from 0 to 6. With each adventure, the hero gains experience points. He can mark this out on the back of the hero sheet. For 5 completed experience points, any ability can be upgraded by +1. Experience points are awarded by the master.

Adventrues in Aros

Name: _____   Age: _____

Sex: _____   Skin color: _____

Race: _____   Class: _____

Weapon: _____   Clothes: _____

Str ⬤⬤⬤⬤⬤⬤   Int ⬤⬤⬤⬤⬤⬤

Dex ⬤⬤⬤⬤⬤⬤   Sta ⬤⬤⬤⬤⬤⬤

Cha ⬤⬤⬤⬤⬤⬤   Mon ⬤⬤⬤⬤⬤⬤

Bag: _____

_____

_____

_____

_____

_____

hero sheet

The hero's maximum health points are entered in the corresponding heart field.

If a hero is wounded, the related damage points are subtracted from the hero's health points. If a hero's health points fall to 0, he first falls into a kind of coma. The hero now has 3x the opportunity to pass a (1 of 3) skill check +2 on stamina. If he passes the stamina check, he wakes up with 5 life points from his coma.

But this coma takes its toll. So the hero must sacrifice 1 experience points after his revive.

If all 3 staminia checks fail, the hero dies. Within a day, the hero can be revived with a phoenix feather. If this is not possible, the hero dies and the player must create a new hero. Heroes fallen into volcanoes, crushed, exploded, or otherwise destroyed cannot be revived.

hero sheet

Heroes' Abilities

SWORD = mele Attack How strong can a hero attack. For each filled point, the hero gains an attack die.

The games uses custom attack dice, you can also use standart 6-sided (D6) dice.

Blank sides (1,2,3 - D6)= mean no damage
range symbol (4,5 - D6)= 1 point of damage
skull (6 - D6)= 2 points of damage.

TARGET SYMBOL = ranged Attack How strong a hero can attack in ranged combat. For each filled point, the hero gains an attack die. Every filled dot stands for 8m/yards. If a hero wants to shoot further, he must make a Dexterity test. This mechanic is also important in a tactical game with board and pieces. Each filled dot shows the weapon range in squares on the game board. 2 circles = 2 squares on the game board.

More about this in the chapter Playing with a game board.

hero sheet

SHIELD (Defense) = The amount of damge reduction. For each filled circle, the player gets 1 die for defense roll. In order to reduce damage, the player must roll a 6 (skull on the custom dice).

Example:
The hero is attacked for 4 damage. With 3 circles filled in, the player can roll 3 dice to defend. The player rolls one six (skull). From the 4 damage, now 1 point of damage gets subtracted, leaving the hero to suffer 3 points of damage.

SHOE (Movement distance) = Each turn, a hero can move a certain distance each turn. For each filled circle, a hero can move 3 units of distance (exact units to be decided before play). A player with 3 circles filled can move 9 units per turn of combat.

If using the gameboard, there is differnt movement distance - since the gameboard is divided into squares, each circle would permit 1 square of movement.

Charactersheet

SCR

Strength = physical strength. How strong is a hero. What can he lift, pull, push, carry, hit etc.

INC

Intelligence = knowledge and wisdom. How clever and well-read a hero is. How well can he recognize and interpret tracks. How high is his emotional intelligence and his intuition.

DEX

Dexterity = dealing with one's own body. How acrobatic is a hero. How nimble his fingers. How well can he climb, do gymnastics or pick locks.

SCA

Stamina = How tough and enduring is a hero. How long can a hero sprint, swim, dive, or hold their breath.

CHA

Charisma = looks and likeability. How pretty or how likeable or how ugly and scary is a hero. Can one beguile, influence, intimidate .

Mon

Monster handling = How well trained is my monster. What tricks or special skills can my monster do? Can it climb through bars and get keys, attack or perform tricks.

Heroes

A hero's basic abilities depend on 2 combined factors.

Heritage, which group of beings does the hero belong to.
Classes, what calling does a hero follow.

All heritages and classes can be combined with each other. The combination of heritage and class results in a basic value of abilities for the corresponding hero.

All races have different starting life points. With 15 marked experience points, the life points increase by +1.

Heritages in Aros

Dwarves - Elves - Humans - Shortlings - Orcs

Charactersheet

Wizards, mages, witches, druids, paladins, and Tieflings can cast magic. To do this, spells must be learned (unlocked).
become. The better you learn a spell, the stronger its magic becomes. Spells are also included Skill points unlocked and improved.

Here, too, you can only use 1 of 2 skill points for a spell per level up.

Not every spell works right away, which is why you have to Spell tests are rolled. Samples will be rolled for skills (intelligence, strength, etc.). The modifier will added to the ability score.

$$\text{Int} \; \bullet\bullet\bullet\circ\circ\circ \quad + \quad \boxed{\begin{array}{c}\text{Int}\\+4\end{array}} \quad = \quad 3+4=7$$

For the spell to succeed, the player must roll a 7 or smaller with the 12-sided die.

Depending on the player's level, he can cast 1 or more spells per hour. A level 1 player can cast 1 spell per hour. A level 2 player can cast 2 spells per hour, etc.

Dwarves

Dwarves are short, broad, and sturdy. These tough and often fierce residents of Aros are characterized by strength and tenacity. Dwarves are exceedingly brave and fearless. Many of them see their vocation in the art of war as warriors or hunters. But thieves and artists have also been seen among the dwarves. Dwarfs often live in underground cities and mines. They dig deep into the mountain. They love gold and precious stones. Dwarves are often grumpy but extremely loyal.

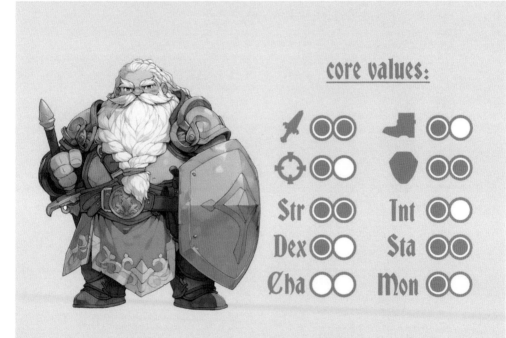

core values:

⚔ ◉◉		🔧 ◉○	
⊕ ◉○		◆ ◉◉	
Str ◉◉		Int ◉○	
Dex ◉○		Sta ◉◉	
Cha ○○		Mon ◉○	

healt points 9

Elves

Elves are often characterized by their connection to animals and nature. They are intelligent and skilled. They have been familiar with handling the bow since childhood. So elves often feel comfortable as hunters and artists. Their high intelligence allows some to become powerful sorcerers. But there are also powerful elven warriors who compensate for their lack of strength with skill. Elves are keen scouts, often spotting their enemies earlier than other races.

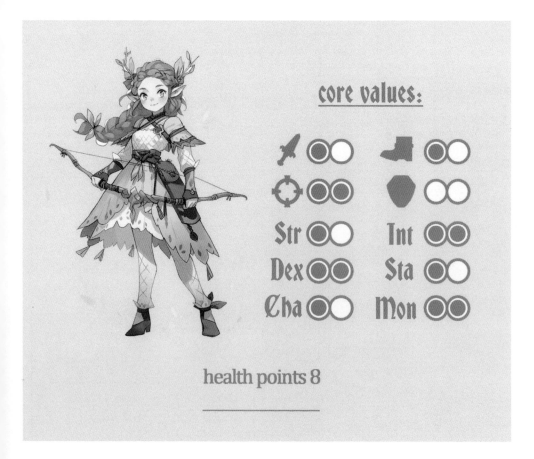

core values:

⚔	◉◉○	👢	◉◉○
🎯	◉◉○	🛡	◉○○
Str	◉◉	Int	◉◉
Dex	◉◉	Sta	◉◉
Cha	◉○	Mon	◉◉

health points 8

Humans

Humans are somewhere between dwarves and elves in terms of their abilities. They aren't as tough and fierce as dwarves, but then again, not as intelligent and gifted as elves. Humans are characterized by an extremely strong will. They have a wide range of talents and can cope well with all professions. Some people are characterized by their love for animals. So there are some very powerful monster tamers among humans.

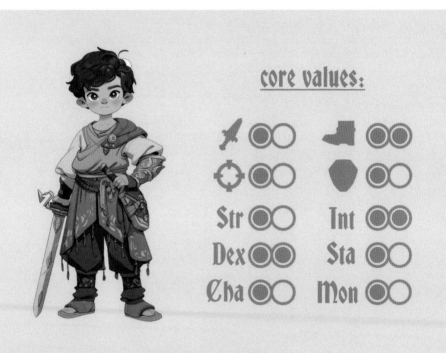

core values:

Str ● ●   Int ● ●
Dex ● ●   Sta ● ●
Cha ● ●   Mon ● ●

health points 7

shadow Elves

Dark Elves are very rare in Aros. You don't talk much about your origins. Characteristics are very calm and thoughtful. Your intelligence is very high, as is your charisma. Anyone who loses themselves in the eyes of a dark elf finds it difficult to lie. When it comes to dealing with animals and monsters, they tend to be calm and intelligent companions like Eulox or foxes. There are powerful magicians, cunning thieves ,and experienced druids among you

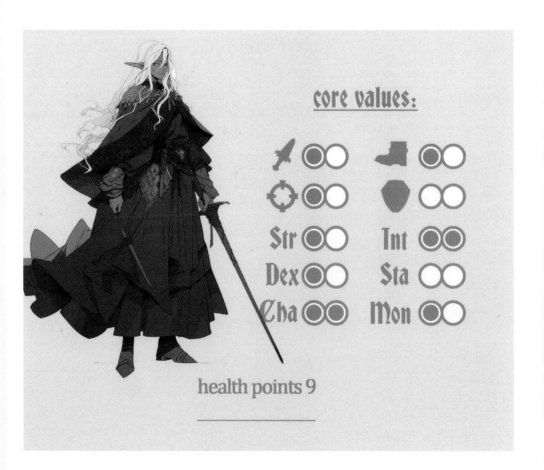

core values:

🗡️ ◉◯	🔺 ◉◯		
◎ ◉◯	🛡️ ◯◯		
Str ◉◯	Int ◉◉		
Dex ◉◉	Sta ◯◯		
Cha ◉◉	Mon ◉◯		

health points 9

Goblins

Goblins are sneaky little fellows. They are very skilled and agile. They are very successful as thieves. No lock or chest is safe from you. Their intelligence is usually not particularly high, which is also reflected in moral questions. Goblins generally cannot be trusted. But not all goblins are like that. There are also honest, friendly ,and open-hearted goblins. But you can never completely give up your love for gold.

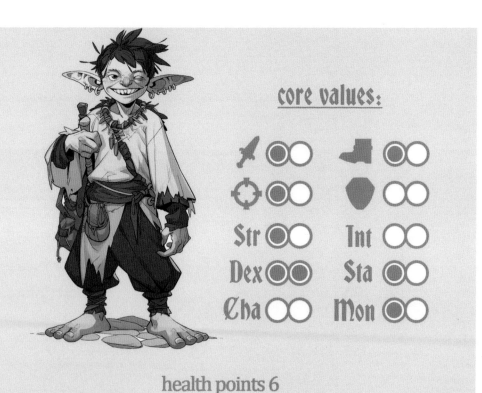

core values:

Str ◉◉   Int ◯◯
Dex ◉◉   Sta ◉◯
Cha ◯◯   Mon ◉◯

health points 6

Beastshaper

Beastshaper are elves with animal-like abilities. You can usually recognize them by small horns, a beak, or a Animal tail. Many of them have the ability to transform into animals or beasts at short notice. Beastshaper are very Close to nature. They usually know very well about plants and fungi. They are excellent as druids, magicians, or hunters. But warriors and thieves have also been seen among them. Beasshaper can't control animals or have pets.

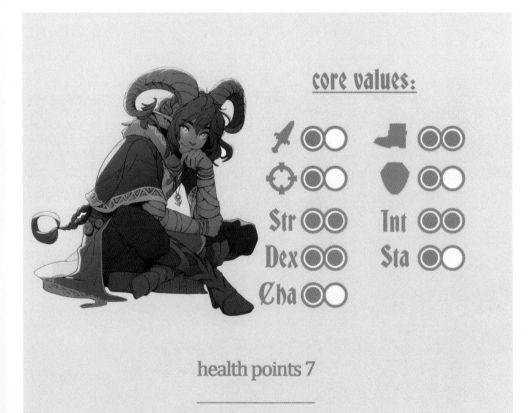

core values:

Str ◉◉ Int ◉◉
Dex ◉◉ Sta ◉◯
Cha ◉◯

health points 7

Shortlings

Shortlings are smaller than dwarves and not nearly as tough as them.
They are characterized by very good skills. Since they can be very quiet,
they are very suitable as thieves and hunters. Shortlings love to read, and
that has produced some great wizards. They are extremely loyal and
friendly. They don't show it, but shortlings can have enormous appetites.
As hungry as they are, they are also brave.

core values:

Str ●○   Int ●●

Dex ●●   Sta ●●

Cha ●○   Mon ●●

health points 6

Orcs

Orcs are hulking and very strong creatures. What they have gained in strength, they mostly lack in intelligence. Their stamina is often inferior to that of dwarves. As warriors, orcs are very dangerous due to their tremendous strength. Orcs move safely and quickly through forests and caves, which has spawned many strong orc hunters. When orcs learn the magic arts, they are often full of corruption.

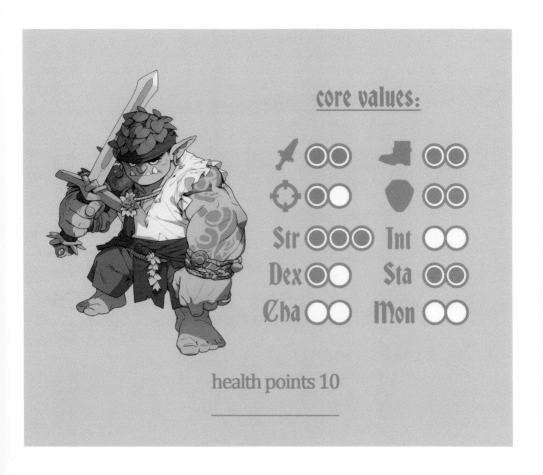

core values:

Str ●●● Int ○○
Dex ●○ Sta ●○
Cha ○○ Mon ●○

health points 10

Classes

Warrior - Hunter - Magician - Thief - Acrobat

Warrior

Warriors are ready for battle. Their whole being and equipment are designed for battle and victory. Warriors often carry heavy weapons. Some of them wear armor or shields, while others go into battle covered only in fur. They don't have a great sense for redundant knickknacks. Efficiency and war suitability is more important. They are keen on the spoils of war, especially stronger or even magical weapons.

class stats:

+2
Str +1

+1
Sta +1

Weapons:
two-handed Warhammer; small Warhammer; Battleaxe, large battle ax (both handed), broadsword, a large mace, two-handed sword, pointed and blunt cutting weapons

Ranger

Rangers have good eyesight. They can spot monsters and enemies very early and take them out silently. Their clothing and armor are light, so they can move well and quickly even in rough terrain. Their dexterity, especially when using long-range weapons and traps, is very good. They often value plants and zoology. Hunters easily find their way in nature. As their intelligence increases, they are sure to recognize medicinal and poisonous plants.

class stats:

◎ +1   Int +1
Dex +1   Mon +2

Weapons:
Shortbow, Longbow, Crossbow, Light Sword, Short Sword
Knife, small axe, throwing axe, spear, slingshot

Thief

Thieves are often devious people. A high charisma helps to beguile or intimidate people to free them from unnecessary treasures or to get important information. Thieves are very good at sneaking, picking locks, and disarming traps. Courage is often their greatest virtue. Some of them have low morale or loyalty. Anyone who trusts a thief too much can easily be deceived.

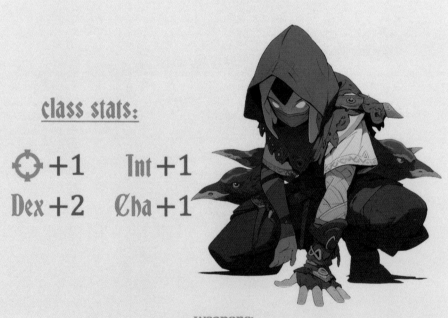

class stats:

⊕ +1   Int +1

Dex +2   Cha +1

weapons:
Knife, throwing knife, short sword, small throwing axe, quarterstaff

Acrobat

Acrobats, jugglers, and actors have very good body control and extraordinary charisma. Your agility and dexterity will help you jump over walls, escape prisons, or charm guards. A permanent home and Commitments are not in their nature. They are open to new things and quickly find new friends.

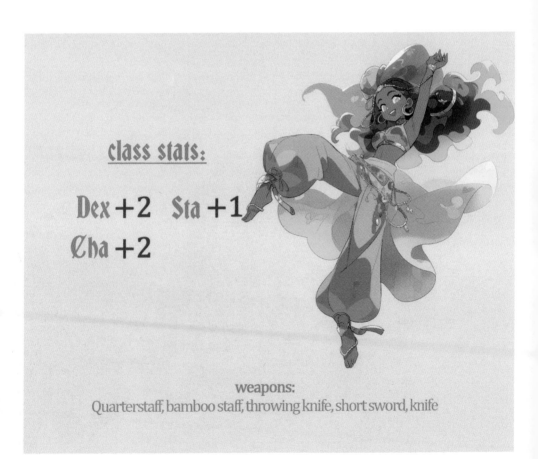

class stats:

Dex +2 Sta +1
Cha +2

weapons:
Quarterstaff, bamboo staff, throwing knife, short sword, knife

Wizards

Wizards, mages, and witches use their intelligence and knowledge to cast spells and manipulate the elements. They wear light clothing or light armor. Wasting energy is unfamiliar to them. Any unnecessary physical strain is avoided (e.g. heavy armor). There are 4 different types of spells in Aros. But all wizards have one thing in common, they start with simple elementary school spells.

class stats:

+1   +2
Int +2

weapons:
Magic Wand, Mage Staff, Small Sword

Game master

Druids

Druids are very close to nature. They have excellent knowledge of plants, fungi, and animals. You can brew various medicinal juices and poisons. Your magical abilities help you cast plant, nature, and weather spells. They can brew juices and cure diseases from even the most inconspicuous things, such as bones or dry plants. Druids are the most powerful magical classes in Aros after mages, sorcerers, and witches.

class stas:

⚔ +1   ⬡ +1
Int +1 Mon +1

Weapons:
Daggers, knives, throwing knives, short swords,
small bow, small crossbow,
wooden stick, wooden stick,

Paladin

Paladins are strong knights who are guided by a divine or spiritual power. This power helps you develop special magical abilities. They use their abilities to protect or heal others. Supported by the energies, they can cast powerful attacks and knock down even the strongest opponents. Paladins are usually very nice and friendly and have a very high level of legal awareness. They don't like injustice at all.

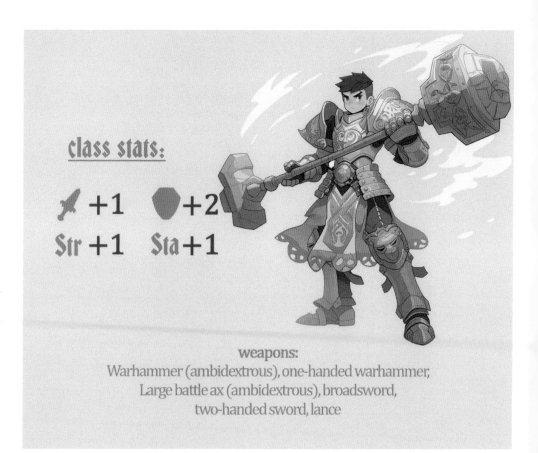

class stats:

+1   +2
Str +1   Sta +1

weapons:
Warhammer (ambidextrous), one-handed warhammer,
Large battle ax (ambidextrous), broadsword,
two-handed sword, lance

Pirate

Sailors and pirates are wild and rough fellows. They know no fear and are usually found on ships far out at sea. But from time to time they go ashore to look for adventure. Sailors are excellent swimmers and are very familiar with all types of boats. Like goblins and thieves, they are cunning and you shouldn't trust them completely. They usually have a great sense of humor and are full of joy in life.

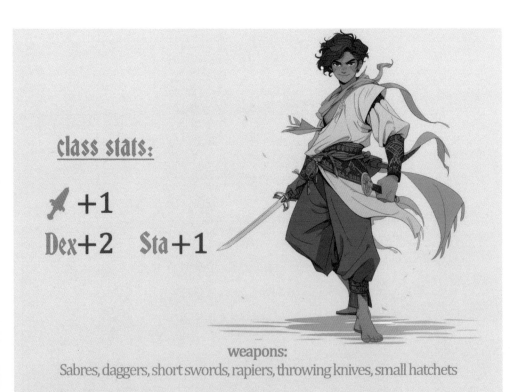

class stats:

+1

Dex +2   Sta +1

weapons:
Sabres, daggers, short swords, rapiers, throwing knives, small hatchets

Game master

The task of the game master is to guide the group through the adventure in the most exciting and unpredictable way possible. No master has ever fallen from the sky. You will only get better by playing often. This way you get a feeling for the individual heroes within a group and the right timing between excitement and relaxation. The game master should not play against the group. Rather, his job is to fill the adventure with life and ideas.

For this, the master has different tools and possibilities. He can test the heroes' abilities through skill checks. Are the heroes even able to turn, what they imagined, into reality? An orc with an Intelligence of 1 will have difficulty reading and understanding a science book. A mage, on the other hand, will not be as skilled with a bow as a ranger.

In order to test the heroes' wishful thinking, the individual abilities of the heroes are rolled on a skill check. The player rolls the 12-sided dice to check his abilities. The aim is to undercut the determined value with the 12-sided dice.

Game master

The master can push heroes harder or give them a hand if things get too wild. In this way, the master can make more attackers appear or allow monsters to ward off damage. In return, however, he can make monsters weaker or incapacitated by unfortunate circumstances. In this way, the master can prevent all of his players from being killed by a monster with too much luck with the dice.

If the master wants to get a group to do something, but they don't respond, there is no point in pushing the group in the desired direction. With a little finesse and the promise of gold and treasure, most heroes can be lured.

Game master

A master does not always have to know everything. Notes can help not to lose the thread or not to overlook important information. As a master, something always goes wrong. The group does the opposite of what you'd expect, the monsters die faster than they should, or the boss lets himself be charmed by a pretty acrobat and abandons his dark plans. The master should let the players have their fun. If the group enjoys converting baddies more than killing them, a good master will join in. The group should have fun. As a master, you can turn the tide at any time and a villain, who was just nice, suddenly shows his true face. This way you can get tension and drama out of even the most unplanned situations.

Improvisation and creativity are important tools when dealing with a group. A good master remains open and relaxed when things don't go as planned. As a master, you always have the opportunity to influence the adventure. If the group takes a wrong turn and is now walking in the wrong direction, you can let a small scruffy bridge collapse and the heroes have to turn back.

skill checks

Since different actions have different levels of difficulty, there are so-called modifiers. The modifier indicates how hard or easy an action is.

The modifier is added to the hero's ability.

Skill checks that can be tested for:

Strength, Intelligence, Dexterity, Stamina, Charisma, Monster

The more experienced heroes become, the more they develop individual skills, the easier it is to pass skill tests. A advanced hero has a higher chance of making a daring move work than a novice. Actions are always checked for the appropriate ability. If a large stone is to be moved, the test is made for strength. If a book in an ancient language is to be deciphered, the Intelligence test is rolled.

skill checks

The following values exist for the difficulty of an action:

very easy: +5
easy: +4
normal: +3
heavy: +2
very difficult: -1
almost impossible: -4

Example:
A hero wants to shoot down a mushroom on a tree trunk 5 distance units away, an effortless task for a ranger. Therefore the modifier is +5

If the hero has a dexterity stat of 3, this stat is increased to 8 because of the +5 modifier. In order to see if the hero's attempt succeeds, a d12 must be rolled by the player. The player must match or undercut 8.

skill checks

The same pinciple applies to negative modifiers. Let us say that the same hero (DEX 3) wants to shoot a gold coin from the claws of a flying monster a significantly farther distance away. Even for a very skilled archer, this would be very challenging; therefore a modifier of -1 would be applied.

-1 is now subtracted from his dexterity of 3. The player must roll a 2 or less to pass the test.

The master decides whether a test should be rolled. Skill checks make the game dynamic and prevent players from getting away with absurd ideas or actions. Skill checks can add realism to the game.

skill checks

Luck and bad luck.

If a player rolls a 1 or a 12, a special rule applies. A 1 on the 12-sided die means special luck. The hero's action not only works, it works particularly well. Usually, there is a small bonus. For example, a hero hits two enemies with one arrow, or he finds a small gold coin under a heavy rock.

The exact opposite happens when the player rolls a 12. Something goes terribly wrong, which usually has negative consequences. The hero shoots himself in the leg and takes damage, or his action fails in such a way that he or the whole party are now in danger. The master decides on bonus or damage. Bonus and damage aren't a must, but they add to the gameplay.

skill checks

interrogate	Cha	run	Sta
arm wrestling	Str / Sta	wrestle	Str
evade	Dex	push	Str
tinker, sew	Dex	hit	Str
beguile	Cha	sneak	Dex / Sta
deceive	Cha	pick locks	Dex
unconscious	Sta	craft	Dex
bend	Str	write	Int
fawn	Cha	swim	Sta
intimidate	Cha	jump	Dex / Str
recognize emotions	Int	steal	Dex
defuse trap	Dex	symbology	Int
to set a trap	Dex	dive	Sta
fall damage	Sta	tame animals	Cha
manual dexterity	Dex	zoology	Int
foreign languages	Int	carry	Str
medicine	Int	do gymnastics	Dex
climb	Dex / Sta	negotiate	Cha
to read	Int	seriously injured	Sta
hold your breath	Sta	throw	Str
botany	Int	weather science	Int
rip out	Str	magick	Int

Experience points

The master awards experience points after completing adventures. These points are collected on the 2nd page of the hero sheet. When 5 experience points are collected, the hero receives 2 skill points that he can distribute between skills, monster skills, and spells.

Both skill points cannot be the same
Ability or spell is distributed.

So a hero 3x5 has collected a number of experience points. If he increases in level by +1, he permanently receives +1 more life points.

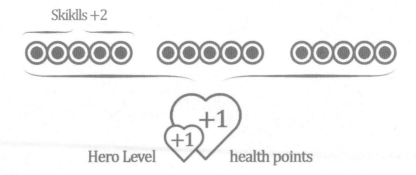

experience points

Experience points can be awarded after an adventure. The amount of experience points depends on the length and difficulty of the adventure.

Usually 3-7 experience points per adventure is a good value. Experienced heroes usually get less than absolute newbies. Beginners and newbies are constantly learning new things, so they can level up faster, which also adds to the fun of the game.

Strong heroes are already well-versed in adventuring and their progress is now a little slower. This can also prevent heroes from becoming too strong too quickly.

Experience points can also be awarded for particularly successful actions or creative ideas. If you show great courage or great concern, you can earn experience points. A roll of 1 on a test can also be rewarded with an experience point. Such small gifts can keep the morale high, but should still be used not too often. Otherwise the players may constantly try to outdo each other in order to get another experience point.

fight order

Battles are fought in alternating rounds. Depending on the situation, the heroes start first or the enemies. If the heroes surprise a group of orcs, the heroes may attack first. If the group is surprised by orcs, the orcs may attack first.

All heroes and their monsters attack one after the other, then all enemies fight back one after the other. Then the next round begins and the whole thing starts all over again. When all opponents are defeated, the fight is over.

This form of combat has the advantage that it is easy to understand. In larger groups of 4 or more players, this can create an imbalance. You can use the 50/50 rule here. Divide the heroes and enemies into 2 halves. First, players 1 & 2 attack, then the first half of the orcs fight back, then players 3 & 4 attack. Then it is the turn of the remaining orcs to attack.

Tip:
It is better to attack with several weaker opponents than one very strong one. This allows each hero to concentrate on one or more opponents, and the heroes are less likely to be killed by a very strong opponent.

combat system

The combat system consists of attack, defense, and special attacks or spells. Each hero has 1 opportunity to move and 1 action per round. Actions are attack, special attack, cast a spell or interact with items. Items, for example, could be using a potion or throwing an object in the environment like a barrel.

Attacks are determined with dice. The attack value corresponds to the sword/range value on the hero sheet.

mele attack   range attack

If a hero has painted 3 dots behind the sword/range, he can attack with 3 dice. Attack dice have 3 different sides.

There are special Aros attack dice, alternatively, you can use normal 6-sided dice.

Blank pages (1,2,3)= mean no damage
Range (4.5) = 1 point of damage
Skull (6)= 2 points of damage.

The damage points rolled are added up and subtracted from the opponent's health points.

combat system

Does a hero have one or more dots behind the shield icon marked, he can try to reduce damage.

To do this, he rolls the number of attack dice he has painted behind the shield symbol. 2 marked circles = 2 dice.

For each skull (6) rolled, the player may subtract one damage dealt by a monster. For example, a monster dealing 4 damage to a hero , he rolls 2 dice. One die is a skull (6) so now he can reduce 1 hitpoint.

combat system

In addition to normal attacks, there are special attacks and special spells. These attacks have a longer range, deal more damage, or give the hero special opportunities to turn the fight in their favor.

Special attacks require skill checks to be rolled (12-sided die). If these are successful, a special attack is carried out. If it fails, the hero cannot attack again that turn. In the next round, the hero can attack either normally or again try a special attack.

Game masters can build treasure chests during the game. These treasure chests can contain gold, items, or magic weapons with unlock special attacks. Special Attacks can be unlocked and upgraded with experience points

special attacks

Special attacks can be unlocked and upgraded with skill points
(5x experience points). To cast the ability, the hero must pass the
appropriate skill check. To use a fire attack, the hero must pass a check.
If a hero has a stat of 2 for intelligence, they must roll a 4 or lower with
the d12. The skill adds 2 on top of the hero's intelligence stat, in this case
2 (the hero INT) + the 2 required by the skill equals a skill check value
of 4. 2 (spell) + 2 (hero) = 4) or lower on the 12-sided die to pass the
test. If the test fails, the hero loses his attack for the round.

If the test succeeds, the hero can carry out the corresponding action.

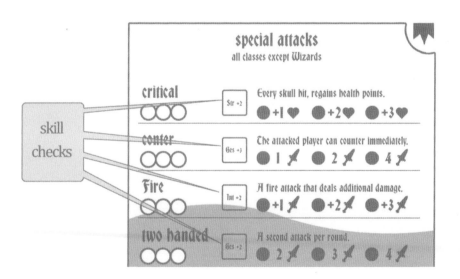

healing

Heroes can be wounded not only in battles but also by events. A failed skill check on dexterity can lead to a climbing fall. The amount of damage is determined by the master. A good base value is 1 point of damage per meter from a height of 4 meters/yards.

If a hero has been damaged, there are several ways to heal.
Pauses can help regenerate health points. Heroes recover 1 health point per hour (in-game - not real) after a break of 2 hours. This means that there is no recovery in the first hour of the break. Long pauses overnight, during which heroes sleep for more than 7 hours, usually restore all health points.

Health potions are another way to regain health points. You can make these yourself or buy them (see White Starthorn – Plants & Fungi). Casters can also pass a skill check for healing spells. If this fails, it can be repeated (1x per round in combat).

develop story

A simple way to create a good story is the beginning-end method. The beginning and end are given. The middle part is worked out and build piece by piece.

Beginning: The group is out in the woods.
End: A daughter returns to her father.

Now you can slowly start to develop the story by starting to ask questions:

Why are the heroes in the forest? (hunt, walk, mission)
Who is the daughter (farmer's, king's, robber's daughter)
Why was she gone? (kidnapped, lost, escaped, etc)
How did the heroes find out about this?(seen, heard, order)
What did the heroes have to do? (liberate, find)

Each answer leads a little bit further into the story. Each answer determines the way forward. In this way, the story writes itself.

develop story

The core of the game consists of a good story. The adventure should be exciting, not too lengthy, and suitable for the group. Developing a good story is easier than you think.

The easiest way to build stories is in 3 acts. A beginning, a middle, and an end. The climax should come at the end of the middle part. Then you have enough time to let the story end slowly.

The adventure should not be too transparent. This means the players shouldn't know what happens next. The easiest way to achieve this is to build small unexpectetd plots twists into the story. So the nice landlord turns out to be sneaky villain.

Stylistic terms should not be repeated too often. If a found key always means that there is a chest nearby, players will adjust to that. This can quickly lead to boredom.

Monsters

There are monsters everywhere in Aros. Some can fly, others burrow through the ground, and others will eat anything they can get their teeth on. But not all monsters are equally dangerous. Some of them can even be downright useful.

If you have the right skills, you can even catch and train monsters. So you have a useful friend not only in battle but also in everyday life. Depending on how clever such a monster is, it can certainly complete demanding tasks.

Monsters have different values. Some monsters are particularly strong, while others are very fast or extremely clever. Don't underestimate little or cute looking monsters. They may look small and weak, but their intelligence can make them quite dangerous.

As a game master, you should incorporate the intelligence and skill of the individual monsters into the adventure. All specified values are basic values and can be adjusted at any time. The game master can strengthen or weaken monsters. So you can make fights and scenarios exciting and great.

Monsters

Below the monster description are the base stats for that monster. The icons show the values for combat scenarios. At the bottom are the values for the skills. Monsters have Strength (Str), Intelligence (Int), Dexterity (Dex), and Stamina (Sta) values.

If a player wants to catch a monster, he must make a skill check on his monster value. The monster's value serves as a modifier. If the player has a value of 2 (on his monster skill), the monster value of the monster is added at + or at - subtracted.

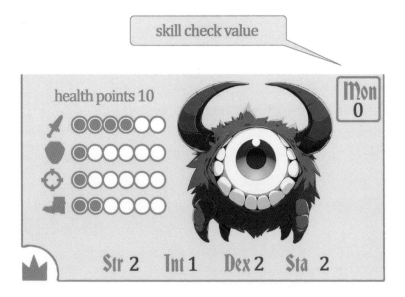

catch monsters

The player has a monster value of 3. If he wants to catch the Horngloop, he must roll a 3 or less on a 12-sided die

Monster 3(player) + Mon 0(monster) = 3

If he wants to catch a skulling he must roll a 6 or smaller on a 12-sided die.

Mon 3(player) + Mon 3(monster) = 6

For each failed test, the player takes one combat die of damage. If he passes the skill check, he caught the monster.

Monster

Each player can only have 1 monster in their possession at a time. If he wants to catch a new monster, he must first release his old monster. Some monsters turn against their former owners.

The game master can decide whether the released monster moves away peacefully or whether it attacks. The gamemaster can also ask for a stamina skill check. The longer the monster has been in the player's possession, the harder the test can be. If the test fails, the monster attacks.

If a player has leveled up his monster, he loses all these experience points. The next caught monster starts again with the default values.

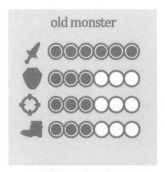

old monster

Old monster values
will not be transferred.

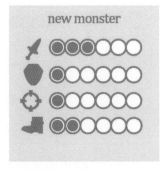

new monster

Monster

Monsters can be played like heroes. They can fight, use their skills, and complete tasks. As with normal heroes, monsters must pass skill tests when they are to be used. Let an Eulox fly through a tower window and steal a key that's on a table. You have to pass as skill check on intelligence and dexterity. The game master decides which tests are rolled and how easy or difficult they are.

The following values exist for the severity of an action:

very easy: +5

easy: +4

normal: +3

heavy: +2

very difficult: -1

almost impossible: -4

As with heroes, the same applies here. If a player rolls a 1 on a test, this succeeds particularly well. This can be rewarded with a bonus or a great promotion. If the player rolls a 12, the test fails miserably. This can result in the monster suffering damage.

monster sheet

Monsters are played like normal players. The monster's basic values are entered on the sheet and can be leveled up with increasing experience. All values and life points can be leveled up.

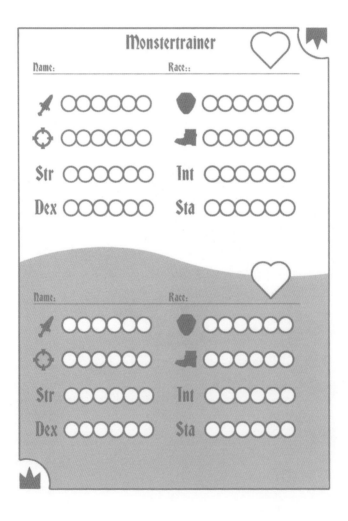

monster attacks

Monsters are played in battle like heroes. Attack, defense, range, and movement stats function the same.

Monsters with an Intelligence of 4 or higher can attack on their own. This means that heroes with a monster can attack twice per turn. The hero has the first attack, the monster has the second attack Monsters with an intelligence below 4 must be directed in battle, which means that the player can only attack once per round. Either he attacks the opponent himself, or he sends his monster into battle.

If a monster dies in battle, it can be revived with a Phoenix Feather. Health potions and medicinal plants have the same effect on monsters as poisons and spells.

If a monster dies and cannot be revived, the player gains 1 experience point. If a player kills their monster on purpose he does not get any experience points.

Monster Tracker

The monster tracker helps the game master to have all attacking monsters and their values available at a glance. All Stats of the monster are added into the monster tracker. So the game master does not have to constantly look up the rulebook to have the individual values at hand.

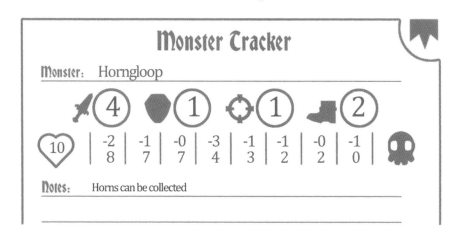

The maximum life points are entered into the heart. The sections adjacent to the heart are where damage is subtracted per turn; the monster is defeated when it has no more life points. The "Notes" section is for any information that might be important or interesting for players. For example, the master can write that a defeated goblin will drop a key or that the group can collect materials (like fur or horns) from monsters.

Puddle Henry

The Puddle Henry is a nasty slime monster. He camouflages himself as a puddle in forests, meadows, and caves. If a creature comes by, it puckers itself up and pounces on its prey. Its sticky consistency gives its poor victims little chance. Its toxic gastric juices decompose their prey in a matter of days, leaving nothing but a pile of bones. Puddle Henrys are easy to spot by their musty smell. Piles of bones left behind indicate that one or more Puddle Henrys have been here. Puddle Henrys are vulnerable to both normal and magical weapons and spells. They are particularly sensitive to extreme heat. Small Puddle Henrys can be caught and tamed in magical bottles. However, they are rather dumb and can only learn simple tasks or attacks.

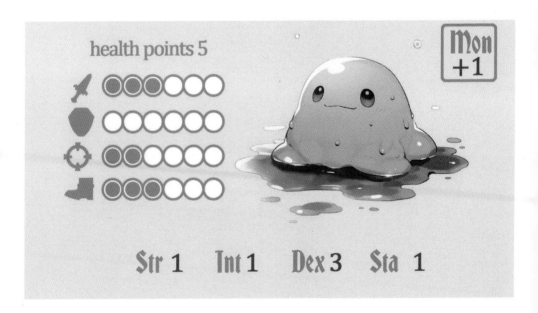

Mountain goat

Mountain goats are very agile, excellent climbers, and of average intelligence; however, they are very tempermental and easily disturbed. They are especially sensitive when it comes to their children. One should not approached their children too closely - under no circumstances should they be annoyed lest they call out to their parents for help. There have been instances where children and sometimes smaller people have been abducted by goats and left alone in meadows or on rocky hilltops. Grass elves are the favorite food of the mountain goat. Their fur and horns can be collected and processed into useful items. Mountain goats can be caught and tamed, serving as mounts for smaller folk.

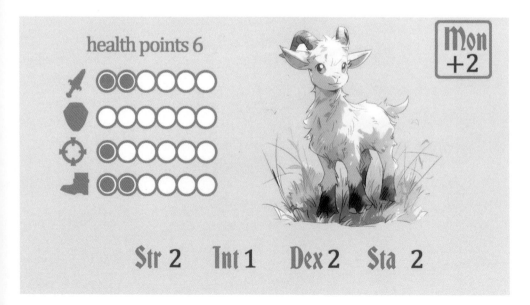

health points 6

Mon +2

Str 2   Int 1   Dex 2   Sta 2

Mimic

A Mimic is a nasty fellow. He can transform himself into an everyday object. Many heroes wanted to open a treasure chest only to find out that it was a nasty mimic. Then, instead of treasures, there is most likely death waiting. Mimics can stay in Disguise for weeks, months, and sometimes even years. They are only able to transform into objects their size. So they cannot shrink or make themselves bigger then they are. Also, the mimic cannot imitate anything living. He likes to disguise himself as a piece of furniture, a barrel, a box, a treasure chest, or a carpet. Mimics can be wounded with normal and magical weapons. Young mimics can be tamed using magic. They can be used as spies or guards. Their intelligence is rather low.

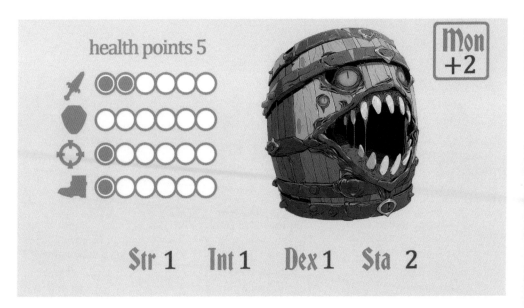

health points 5

Mon +2

Str 1   Int 1   Dex 1   Sta 2

grass elves

There are many stories of grass elves helping humans, elves, dwarves, or other creatures out of trouble. Their biggest threat are mountain goats. So if you mess with mountain goats or even defend a grass elf, you can be sure of their friendship. However, one should not underestimate them. The older ones in particular have magical powers that when combined can cause enormous damage. Their spells inflicted burns on the skin like a thousand nettles. But they also have healing powers they can use to heal themselves or other allies. Anyone who receives a grass elf mask as a gift can count themselves lucky. You will only get an elf mask if you provide a great service or protection to them. Grass Elves can be befriended but not tamed.

health points 10

Str 1   Int 4   Dex 4   Sta 1

Zombie

Every zombie was once a normal citizen who became a zombie through magic or disease. Even the nicest and most decent people are intolerable as zombies. They stink, burp, and bite like crazy. Zombies attack humans, elves, halflings, dwarves, and orcs alike. They love brains and guts so they will have no mercy. If you've been bitten by a zombie, you might transform into one very soon. However a special medicine or magic spells can heal you before you turn into one. Zombies are slow but like to appear in groups. They react to loud noises, light, and hasty movements. The more you stink, the less noticeable you are around zombies. Since zombies are creatures of instinct, they cannot be tamed or befriended.

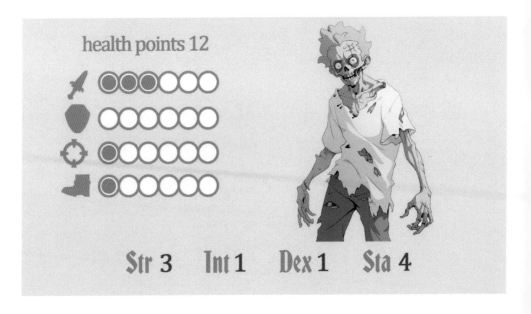

health points 12

Str 3   Int 1   Dex 1   Sta 4

Skully

Skullys are what's left of zombies after a long time. When the body and everything around it have rotted away, only the skull remains. These skulls jump across the ground by snapping their jaw open and shut. They are fearless and might even attack full-grown Orcs. Luckily a bite from a skully won't turn you into a Zombie. However, the bite is not less painful. Also, skulllys appear in groups, making them very dangerous. They jump around like a bunch of fleas, attacking their prey from all directions. One powerful swipe is enough to turn a skully into a pile of bone meal. Skullys are very stupid but can be tamed. Once tamed they can only attack. They are just not smart enough for more demanding tasks.

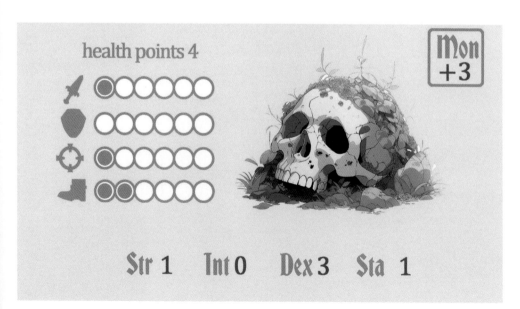

health points 4

Mon +3

Str 1   Int 0   Dex 3   Sta 1

Fluffball

There's a fluffy ball flying through the darkness hunting for blood. It can only be a fluffball. Those cute-looking Bats are smart and dangerous. The older they get, the smarter and more fierce they become. Fluffballs can fly completely silently. You usually don't hear them coming. They can appear in swarms but are often found alone. They attack their prey from midair and often cause bad wounds with their sharp teeth. Young bats are easy to tame. They remain loyal to their trainers for life, even after a long separation. They become very intelligent in old age. Once tamed they can learn a bunch of tricks and attack very aggressively.

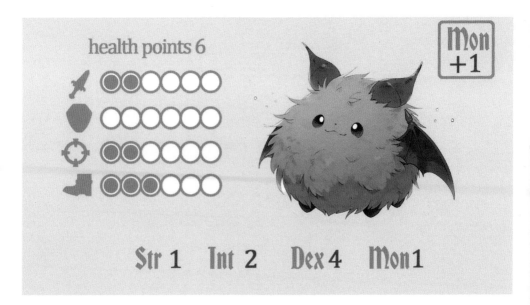

fake Glooper

Gloopers are extremely dangerous. The fake glooper, however, is not only dangerous, it is even fatal in most cases. Fake Gloopers look like normal Gloopers at first glance. But their temperament is much meaner. They are very aggressive and always driven by hunger or bloodthirst.. Unlike real Gloopers, they feed on flesh, blood, and bones. Their eyes will also see you in the dark. They have great night vision. Their big mouth is spiked with razorsharp teeth. They will chew on any and everything that fits inside. Once they fixate their prey, it's hard to get away. Fake Gloopers flee very rarely. They usually fight to the death. They can be killed with conventional weapons or spells. Fake Gloopers cannot be tamed.

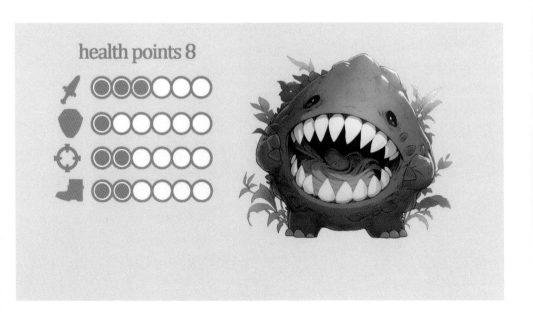

health points 8

Skeletons

Skeletons are dead people who are kept alive beyond their death by a spell or magical task. They are fearless fighters who don't know fear, cold, hunger, exhaustion or pain. They either faithfully follow their task or simply attack everything that approaches them. Skeletons tend to be skilled fighters that are not easy to defeat. However, their intelligence is very limited. Without a brain, thinking is a bit difficult. But you shouldn't underestimate them. Skeleton warriors come in all varieties, even ranger and crossbow varieties have been seen. Although they no longer have eyes, they hit purposefully their opponents. Skeletons cannot be tamed. However, skeletons who serve a magical task can become friends if you support them in their task.

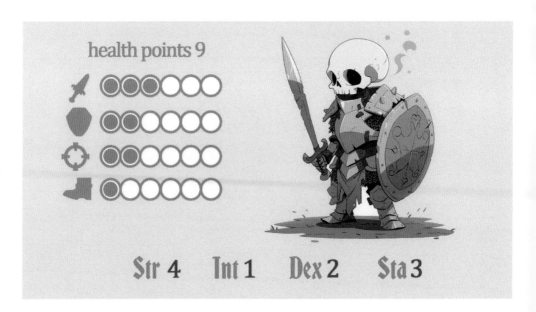

health points 9

Str 4   Int 1   Dex 2   Sta 3

spiders

Young spiders can look very cute. Their big bulging eyes seem almost too adorable. However, you should not be fooled by them. Spiders are swift hunters and show no mercy. Especially in a siblings group they are jealous of food and therefore extremely dangerous. They can spin sticky webs from which even strong dwarves or orcs can hardly escape. Mother spiders are a nightmare come true. They're big, not particularly pretty, and always on the hunt for food for their little ones. Spiders can be found in forests, caves and ruins. You can tame young spiders and bind them to yourself. They are clever and can learn numerous tricks. Spiders are extremely loyal to their owners. However, if they come into contact with their biological siblings, they quickly throw their loyalty aside in favor of their biological brethren..

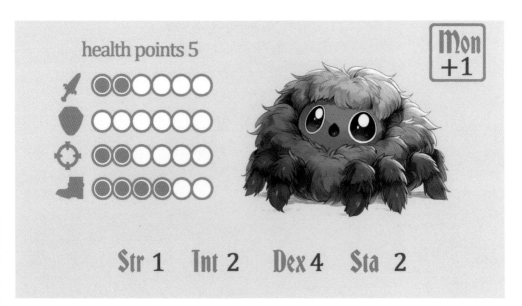

Glooper

The Glooper is a semi-magical being. It feeds on light, which it sucks in with its eye. Gloopers are extremely sensitive and feel disturbed by even the smallest things. If you disturb them, they might attack you immediately. Horngloopers try to impale troublemakers with their horns. Rockgloopers might ram you with their rock hard skulls. Gloopers live mostly alone and mainly found in forests or meadows with tall grass (Hornglooper) or in rocky deserts and caves (Rockglooper). Gloopers can run very fast on their 3 legs and are extremely agile. They are very intelligent, but also very spirited and sensitive. Gloopers can be tamed. They can follow orders and attack, but their temperament can easily distract them or lure them into a trap.

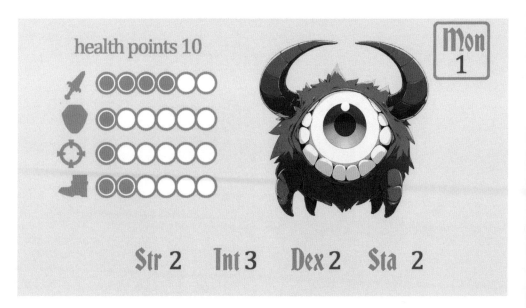

Earthgrup

The Earthgrup is a nasty worm that lives deep underground, just
waiting for something to move above. When heroes or animals run
across his territory, he shoots out of the ground and grabs what he can
get. The Earthgrup is an omnivore and makes no difference between
humans and mice. Since you never know where he is, you should walk
very quietly and carefully through his territory. You can tell if he is
nearby by the large mounds of earth it piles up or the holes it leaves
behind. He devours small victims with one bite or grabs larger victims
and pulls them into his kingdom deep underground. Here he creates
huge labyrinths of passages and chambers. He can be defeated with
weapons and spells. Earthgrup can be caught with large fishing hooks,
rope, and bait. But they cannot be tamed.

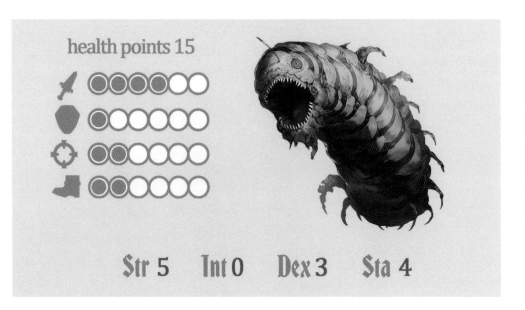

health points 15

Str 5   Int 0   Dex 3   Sta 4

Raptor

Dinosaurs are very rare in Aros. Now and then a small population might be seen in an abandoned area. Raptors live together in smaller packs. They hunt together and are extremely intelligent. Once they have their prey in sight, they might track it down or follow it for a long time. Due to their enormous speed and intelligence, they are difficult to defeat. Young raptors can be caught easily, but they are strongly defended by the pack. If an egg or a youngling is stolen, the pack mercilessly hunts the kidnapper. Eggs can be hatched; this greatly increases the bond between the Rapor and his trainer. Raptors can be trained very well because of their intelligence. They also serve as mounts for smaller and medium-sized creatures.

health points 14

Mon -2

Str 3   Int 3   Dex 3   Sta 3

eyeslurper

If you want to keep your eyes, you shouldn't get too close to an Eyeslurper. These little nimble beasts are after your eyes. They jump in their victim's face and try with all their might to get their eyes. With a powerful suck, they transport the eye straight from the head into their belly. Eyeslurper is small and rather weak, but extremely quick and sneaky. Despite their rather low intelligence, some Eyeslurpers can speak and think for themselves. Talking Eyeslurpers can become friends and can join a group permanently. Eyeslurpers do not survive in captivity. That's why they can't be tamed.

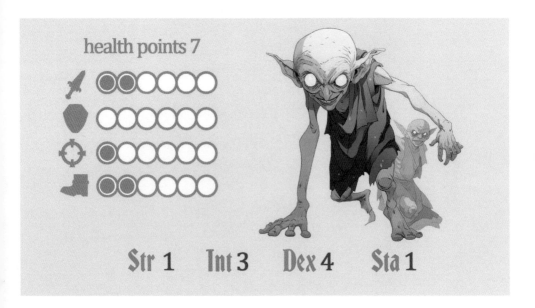

health points 7

Str 1   Int 3   Dex 4   Sta 1

Shog

The Shog is a crossbreed between a shark and a frog. He's a freak of nature. The Shog can swim at lightning speed. On land, he jumps to get around. The Shog is a solitary animal and can be found on coasts and beaches, but also in puddles and swamps. He feels equally comfortable in fresh and salt water. His razor-sharp teeth are very dangerous. With a well-aimed bite, he can bite off hands and feet. Anyone encountering a Shog should beware. They jump at you and create huge wounds with their teeth. Some Shogs have small rockets tied to their backs, giving them greater distance at the expense of a lifespan cut short by detonation. Which evil genius is doing this, is still unknown. Maybe this secret will be revealed one day. The Shog can be caught and tamed. It usually serves as a battle animal, since its intelligence is rather low.

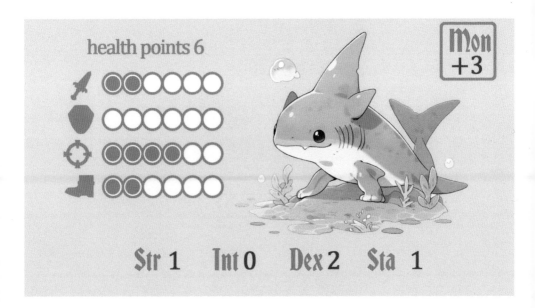

health points 6

Mon +3

Str 1   Int 0   Dex 2   Sta 1

Blueberry octopus

Giant blueberries are very popular in Aros. Its sweet taste and light healing properties are very popular. The blueberry octopus lives between these blueberries. At first glance it looks like a giant blueberry. But if you take a closer look, you will discover the small tentacles and their cute bulging eyes. Blueberry octopuses are usually very peaceful and loving. They can live both on land and in fresh water. Blueberry octopuses are very intelligent and can be easily caught and tamed. Blueberry octopuses can heal minor injuries.

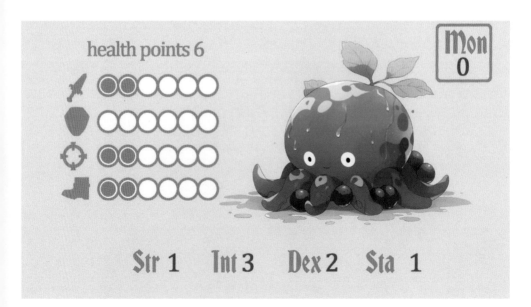

health points 6

Mon 0

Str 1   Int 3   Dex 2   Sta 1

Jelly Johnny

It looks like Jell-O but doesn't taste like it. Jelly Johnny is cute but dangerous. This wobbly monster knows no friendship and is always looking for food. It absorbs food through its skin and digests it inside. He's not particularly picky. The Jelly Johnny digests everything that fits into his body. Unlike the Schlyrp, however, it digests very slowly. You can still discover the remains of their victims in their bodies for months. Some Jelly Johnnys have valuable objects or weapons inside. Which always makes him the target of attacks. But he knows how to defend himself. Once you get stuck, you usually lose your life. Jelly Johnny can be caught and tamed. But their intelligence is rather low.

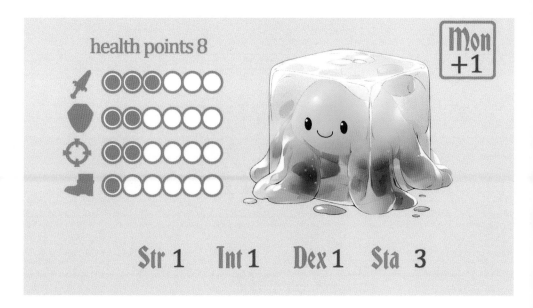

health points 8

Mon +1

Str 1   Int 1   Dex 1   Sta 3

Dragon Isopod

The dragon isopod is a tough and dangerous fellow. His armored skin is very difficult to penetrate. When threatened, he can curl up like a ball. As a ball, it is almost invulnerable (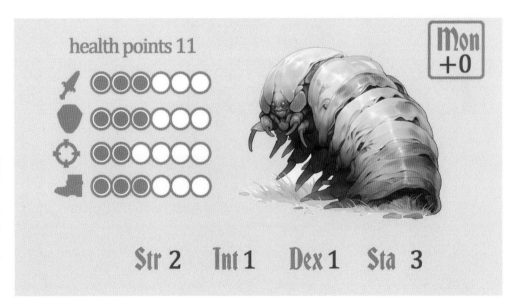 rises to 5) and can withstand even great heat. The dragon isopod has even been seen rolling over small lava fields. It either attcks his opponents as a ball, trying to knock them over with great force, or it rears up and attacks with their claw-like feet. Young dragon isopods are easy to catch and tame. Adult isopods can carry heavy loads on their backs. Their generally calm and down-to-earth nature makes them very popular as animal companions. A true relationship with your companion may last a lifetime. Dragon isopods can live for over 100 years.

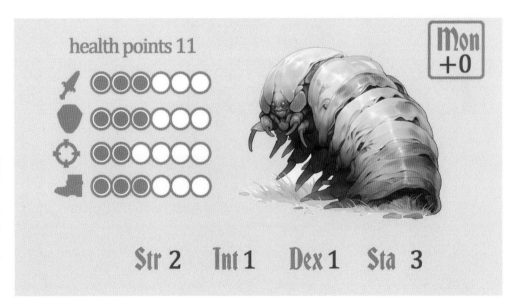

Coral Crabs

Coral crabs live on beaches and between rocks in seas. These beautiful and often colorful animals are beautiful yet very dangerous. In addition to her crab claws, with which she can pinch iron without any problems, she has a paralyzing poison. Immobilized and paralyzed prey is then eaten while fully conscious by a group of hungry coral crabs. Not a nice way to die. They can be found in both salt and fresh water. Coral Crabs can be caught and tamed. The older and larger they are, the more difficult it becomes to bind them to a mate. They have good intelligence and can make independent decisions. In combat situations, they can paralyze and incapacitate opponents. If the coral crab has a close bond with its companion, you can take poison from it to create poison weapons or arrows.

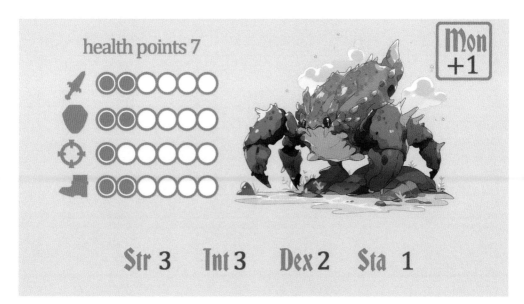

Cricket

You ugly cricket. That's what children in Aros say when they argue. The cricket is a large grasshopper with mighty jaws. Crickets can jump very far due to their strong legs and hidden wings. Their bite is very powerful and their hunger is enormous. Crickets attack alone or in groups. In larger swarms, they can cause enormous damage. Crickets can get very old and therefore grow very slowly. Initially very small, Crickets can grow as large as small horses when they mature. They can be used as draft animals or mounts. Young crickets can be tamed by offering them white damp grass to eat. However, these grasses are very rare and can only be found in a few light-colored forests in Aros. If the Cricket is tamed, it is faithful and will stay with its companion until the end of its life.

rocky Shlurph

Similar to the furry shlurph, the rocky shlurph also has
telekinetic powers. While he cannot teleport, he can lift objects only
using the power of his mind. In nature, the rocky shlurph uses stones
and smaller rocks to defend itself. He lifts them with his telekinetic
powers and then hurls them at his enemies. The rocky shlurph can be
found in mountains and rocky areas. It can be tamed like the furry
Shlurph but has a bit of character. He is more scratchy and less clingy
than the furry Shlurph.

health points 10

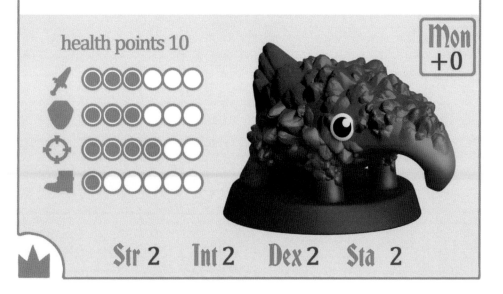

Mon +0

Str 2   Int 2   Dex 2   Sta 2

Slyrp

"Beware of the Slyrp; trust me, this is true! Before you know what happened, he will devour you!" This old rhyme is as relevant as ever. The Slyrp is a nasty slime monster. It will digest anything it can fit in its sticky mouth. It doesn't matter whether it's bone, stone, metal, or wood. The Slryp digests everything. Slyrps like dark and damp corners the most. That's why they are usually found in mines, cellars, caves, or dark forests. They attack silently. They can spit stinking acid, which makes them dangerous even at longer ranges. Slurps move by crawling so they aren't particularly fast. They are difficult to kill as their slimy body can heal wounds very quickly. Of all tameable monsters, the Slyrp is certainly the most useful. He recycles all leftovers and also serves as a living vacuum cleaner.

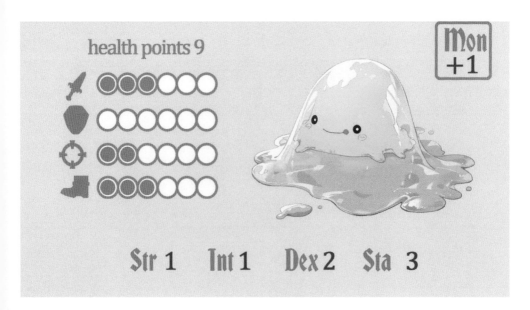

health points 9

Mon +1

Str 1   Int 1   Dex 2   Sta 3

Firemonster

The Firemonster is a living evil. He is a magical creature of fire that consumes everything he can get his burning fingers on. He doesn't stop at living beings either, and his flames devour everything. It is often seen near volcanoes. Firemonsters are difficult to defeat. Of course, their greatest weaknesses are water and ice. They can also be defeated by extinguishing them, like burying them under sand or dirt. If you want to defeat them, you don't need strength, you need brainpower and great ideas. They can be tamed and transported safely in a fire flask. They can be used very well as combat helpers and fire starters. They can hardly learn tricks due to their fiery temperament.

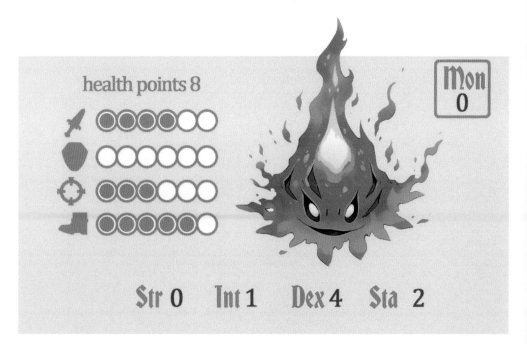

health points 8

Mon 0

Str 0   Int 1   Dex 4   Sta 2

Slimy Eye

Slimy eyes are disgusting slimy eyes on 2 legs. Their pupil is surrounded by teeth. Slimy eyes are extremely quick and agile. They prefer to stay in dark and damp corners of dungeons, caves and cellars. They like to ambush in small groups. They eat everything. They don't scorn carrion either. Slimy eyes defend their prey and are extremely aggressive. They can be defeated with weapons and spells. Their agressive temper makes them untameable.

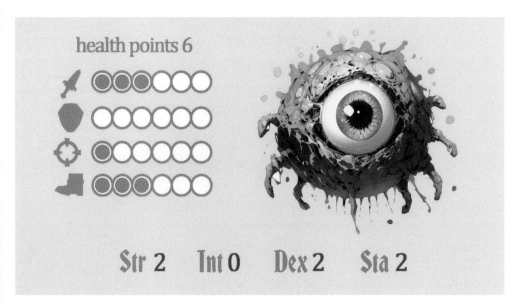

health points 6

Str 2   Int 0   Dex 2   Sta 2

wild Stump

Deep in the damp woods lives the wild stump. Disguised as a tree stump, he waits for his prey in darker corners of forests. Anyone who gets too close will be attacked and eaten without warning. Poisonous mushrooms grow on their bark, which can also be used for special potions. Getting these mushrooms is extremely difficult as the wild stump is an aggressive predator. Its thick bark protects it very well against attacks with weapons. If you want to defeat him you should use fire magic. The wild stump can be caught as a young seedling and kept as a pet. It is not suitable as a battle animal, as it is extremely slow and lazy.

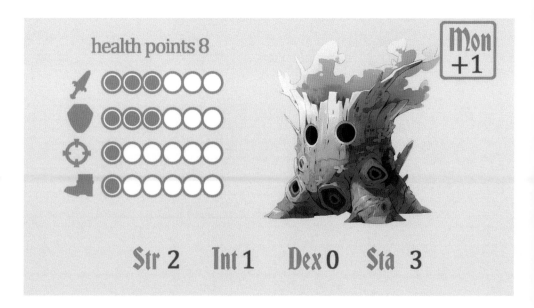

health points 8

Mon +1

Str 2   Int 1   Dex 0   Sta 3

Fox

A fox is an excellent companion. Foxes live in forests and meadows and are usually rather shy. They do not attack larger beings. Their high intelligence and smart skills make them excellent hunters. They can see very well even at night. Their sense of smell is very keen. Young foxes can be trained very easily. They serve as skillful helpers and friends. Against smaller enemies, they can be very suitable as fighting mate. Adult foxes cannot be tamed, but can be befriended.

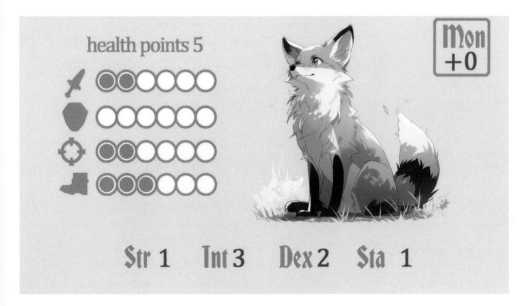

health points 5

Mon +0

Str 1   Int 3   Dex 2   Sta 1

Stonemaw

Just a moment ago there was a stone and suddenly you stare into an open maw. The Stonemaw is a master of disguise. It looks like a big rock that can lie still for months and years. In the right moment, he opens his mouth and snaps. Its enormous biting power stops at nothing. It can even bite through bone and metal without any problems. Since you never know if a Stonemaw is nearby, you should be on guard when traveling through rocky areas. Stonemaws cannot be tamed. Their stubborn and immobile nature renders them virtually useless.

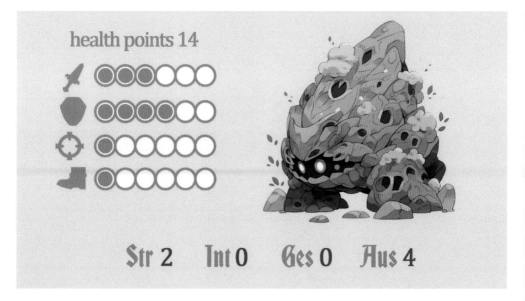

health points 14

Str 2   Int 0   Ges 0   Aus 4

Banana Tucan

This beautiful yellow bird looks very similar to a banana. That's how he got his name. Banana Tucans live on coasts and beaches and are usually very smart. They live in larger groups. Their Intelligence is very high, but their character tends to be devious and mean. One should approach them with caution. Since they don't like troublemakers, they attack quickly. They are sneaky, and mean and will also terrorize other animals. They can be caught and tamed. However, they do not completely lose their nasty and insidious nature even in captivity. So they play pranks on their owners or their friends again and again.

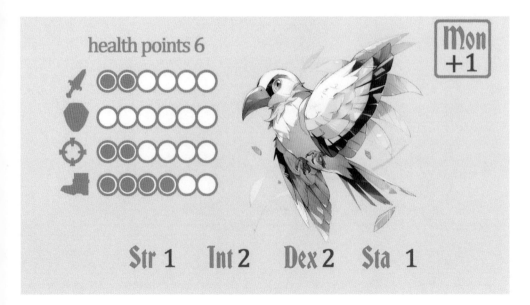

health points 6

Mon +1

Str 1   Int 2   Dex 2   Sta 1

Eulox

The Eulox is a hybrid of an owl and a fox. This feathered animal has the wisdom of the owl and the resourceful cunning of the fox. Eulox can be very dangerous as they can use their superior intelligence extremely skillfully in battle. They can fly silently, see very well in the dark, and have a distinctive sense of smell. Eulox are loners, but that doesn't make them any less dangerous. They watch their prey and often strike unexpectedly from an ambush. Eulox breed in burrows high on rocks or snow-free mountaintops. Whoever approaches their cave nest will regret it very quickly. Eulox can only be tamed by obtaining and raising them as eggs. Nothing can separate the connection between a Trainer and a Eulox. The Eulox will do anything to defend its Trainer. Due to its great intelligence and wisdom, the Eulox is a great animal companion.

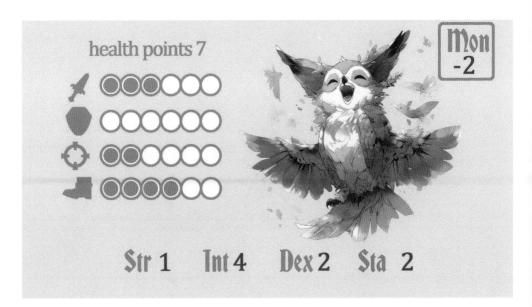

health points 7

Mon -2

Str 1   Int 4   Dex 2   Sta 2

Pumpkin crawler

Pumpkin patches are generally rather dangerous places, even if they don't look like it at first glance. If you don't fall victim to a pumpkin spider, there is still the pumpkin crawler who will try to kill you. An encounter with this monster is not very pleasant. Before you know it, the Pumpkin crawler will bite you in the leg, or its tendrils will grab and squeeze you. Pumpkin crawlers can grow very large and use their mighty tendrils to catch even large animals and monsters. They use their tendrils to move and even climb. The Pumpkin Crawler can be tamed as a young plant. After a certain age and size, however, it can no longer be controlled. So the paths of the trainer and crawler will usually separate after a few years. A young plant can be transported very well. Their moderate intelligence makes them good fighters, but their abilities to learn new tricks is limited.

health points 5

Mon +1

Str 2   Int 1   Dex 1   Sta 2

furry Shlurph

The furry Shlurph is a cute fellow. With its long snout, it looks for small animals and insects on the forest floor. Generally he is rather calm and harmless. He is usually rather shy and will run away when larger animals or monsters approach. But don't underestimate the Shlurph. He has telekinetic powers that he can use in battle or distress. The furry Shlurph can teleport within a medium radius, constantly changing its position. He uses his good intelligence to confuse his opponents and then attack from an unexpected angle. The furry Shlurph can be tamed. He is trusting and loyal as one would expect of dogs. His powers make him very useful in adventures. Its attack strength is rather low.

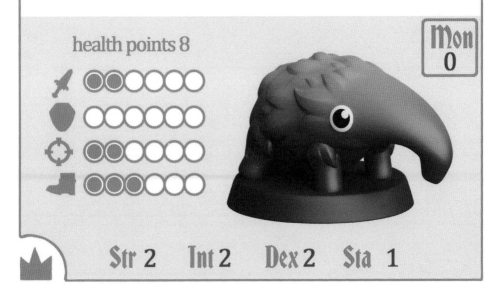

health points 8

Mon 0

Str 2   Int 2   Dex 2   Sta 1

Deathhealer

Just when you think you're saved because you found a healing potion, it turns into a death healer and the end seems near.

Death healers are poisonous gas monsters that hide in healing bottles and wait for prey. If you open or break the bottle, a cloud of poisonous gas will come out and attack you immediately. Death healers can be attacked with weapons and spells. Once out of the bottle, they won't let go of their victims. Ice spells are particularly dangerous for them. Then they freeze into a block and can be smashed. Fire spells should be avoided, as fire will make them even bigger and more dangerous.

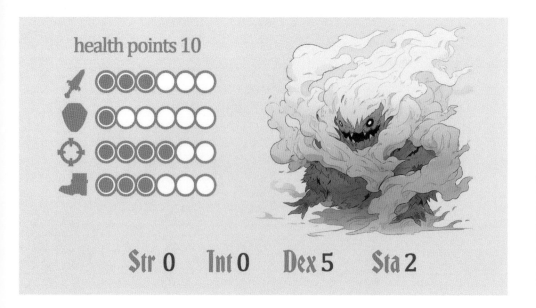

health points 10

Str 0   Int 0   Dex 5   Sta 2

Pumpkinspider

Many farmers have fallen victim to its poisonous bite. At first glance, the pumpkin spider looks like a beautiful ripe pumpkin. But the next moment it shows its true form. Then it is usually too late. Pumpkin spiders have short legs and are rather slow for spiders. But their poison is even deadlier. They often hide between ripe pumpkins and wait for their victims. Pumpkin spiders are solitary and very rarely come in smaller groups. They can be caught and tamed. As a battle pet, they are rather slow but cause additional damage poison damage. Their poison can also be used on arrows and other weapons.

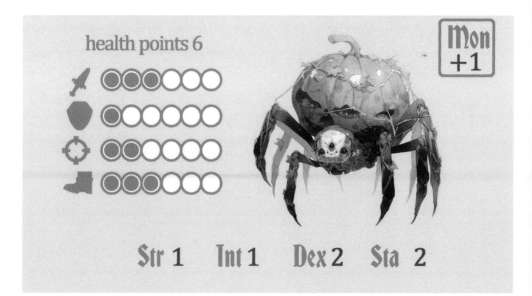

Places

Aros is still an undiscovered world. So far there are only a few described places. Yet the best cartographers, adventurers, and Explorers are already on their way to exploring new areas.

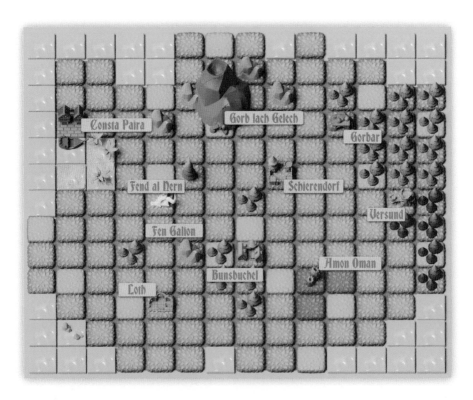

Versund

Versund is the last town in the east. It is a special place. On one hand, Versund lies on the border of two forests, on the other hand, Versund has the largest library of weather and nature spells in all of Aros. The two forests are called Borger Forest and Norger Forest.

These two forests could not be more different. Like two completely different twins. One peaceful, beautiful, full of life and light, the other dead, dark and dangerous. The finest and best woods in all of Aros comes from the Borger Forest. Most citizens of Versund work as lumberjacks, carpenters, or carvers. The fine wood from the Borger Forest is delivered from Versund to all of Aros by ox carts. Wood from the Borger Forest can be recognized by its slightly reddish color and even grain. This wood is processed into all kinds of fine furniture. Tables, chairs, cupboards, and shelves made of Borger wood have been seen all over Aros. Crates and barrels made from this wood last longer than crates made from other types of wood. Therefore, it is often used for treasure chests or barrels for fine wines or goods. Even fruit and vegetables last longer in Borger wood barrels.

The wood from the Norger forest, on the other hand, is useless. It is black, hard as stone, and molds very quickly. Food in barrels made of Norger wood spoils within hours and becomes inedible.

Versund

There are around 80 houses in Versund, including residential houses, a butcher, a bakery, a school, a large tavern with 20 guest rooms, carpentry and the old tower.

This tower is in the center of Versund and in earlier times it served as a watchtower. But now a powerful and already very old wizard lives in it. Gandolin Master of pranks, jokes and stupid ideas, by this name he is known throughout Aros. Gandolin is a master of weather and nature magic. He moved into the tower a long time ago. He lives on the ground floor and he has set up a decent library on the first floor. In this library there are well over 1000 books about plants, herbs, roots, nature and weather magic. He has written over 200 books himself. Most deal with the plants, herbs and roots of the Borger Forest.

But he also wrote a book about the poisonous and deadly plants of the Norger Forest. However, this book was banned because it would be too dangerous if this knowledge fell into the wrong hands. This book is called Magnal Gorgash. Because in the language of the orcs the Norger forest is called Gorgash.

Versund

Versund is surrounded by a palisade fence made from Borger oak. These very tall stakes have been sharpened at the top and serve as protection for Versund. Orcs, goblins, and all kinds of nasty fellows from the Norger forest tried to raid Versund several times in the past. But since Gandolin lives in Versund, the orcs have only dared to attack Versund twice. Each time, however, they were stopped by Gandolin. Versund has not been attacked for 50 years. But Gandolin is growing old and weak. Hopefully, the orcs won't take advantage of that at some point.

Outside Versund's walls flows the little Mehlan, a small river. Here is the house of Brenn the carpenter. He has a small mill on the rapids. Its water wheel drives a saw to cut boards.

The people of Versund are open and friendly towards strangers. The many traders and wood buyers from all over Aros ensure a cosmopolitan flair. There is hardly any crime in Versund. A couple of stolen apples at the weekly market is probably the worst thing that has happened in Versund lately. All in all, Versund is a peaceful and quiet place.

Borger Forest

The Borger Forest is full of life, wonder, and love. It stretches from the north coast of Aros to Versund. Nobody knows where it ends in the east. No one has ever crossed it or flown over it.

The Borger Forest is friendly and full of life. The sun shines on it even more golden and even on rainy days, everything looks happy and boisterous. All the trees and plants are in bloom and it just seems like it's spring all year round. Borger oaks are the largest and thickest trees in all of Aros. The trunk of such an oak tree can grow as large as an entire house. If you hollowed it, a whole family could live in it. An oak tree can grow 30 men high and its canopy stretches like a sky full of leaves high above the forest floor. The Borger Forest is full of oak, birch, maple, pine, and sometimes even willow.

Everything beautiful and peaceful grows and thrives here. Hundreds of various herbs, mushrooms, and berries can be found and collected here. None of it, not a berry or a mushroom is poisonous or inedible. Everything that grows here is healthy and healing or simply delicious. Some mushrooms grow so large that they are considered children could use them as umbrellas. Their golden caps gleam in the morning light when the dew is still fresh. If you like mushrooms, you won't go home empty-handed in the Borger Forest.

Borger Forest

Those with a sweet tooth are more likely to fall for the berries. Wild strawberries, raspberries, blackberries, and giant blueberries are found in abundance.

If you are looking for a rare medicinal plant, you will surely find it in the Borger Forest. Everything that heals, relieves pain, and makes life easier grows and thrives here. Sun clover nettles, snails, white stars and curled moss can also be found just like light violets and meadow ferns are.

The Borger forest is also whimsical. If you have collected berries from a bush and turn around briefly, it can suddenly be full of berries again. Or the bush has suddenly disappeared completely or a different bush suddenly stands in his place. Weren't there mushrooms just now? Now they have disappeared or they are suddenly somewhere else.

That's why the forest is also dangerous, in its way. If you go too deep in, you might not find your way out. You will certainly not starve and die of thirst, but you may not see his home again. That's why even the most experienced dare to venture just a little. Lumberjacks don't have to go far, because the trees they cut down yesterday are miraculously back in their place the next day.

Borger Forest

This forest is a veritable treasury of riches, providing timber and herbs to the people of all of Aros.

If you like watching animals, you will surely discover one or the other animal here. Eulox and blueberry octopus can be found here as well as Grass Elves and Foxes. Many clever animals and monsters live here. All are peaceful as long as you leave them alone. If you are looking for arguments and trouble, this is not the place for you.

This place seems to have something against evil and meanness. Orcs, goblins, and all sorts of other monsters can´t be found here. If such a nasty fellow got lost in this forest, he was never seen from then on. As if the forest floor had simply swallowed him up.

Norger Forest

Eternal night reigns here. The Norger Forest is dark, damp, musty, and full of malice. The trees seem to have faces. Their slender branches are like fingers reaching out for you. Black spruces grow densely here and supress any light.

It's rotting and moldy in every nook and cranny. Poisonous mushrooms grow in damp and musty places. Some of them are filled with vile gases. When touched, they emit poisonous clouds that suffocate all life. Spitting and smacking mushrooms of disgusting slime drip from the trees. If you're not careful, you can even get bitten by a fungus, because some of them have teeth. Disgustingly sharp teeth, dark brown and yellow, full of mucus and bacteria.

Everything that grows here is evil, mean, and poisonous. Ever sleeps, ghost eyes, death singers, and grappling ferns grow here. Deadly herbs and plants for poison potions and dark spells can be found here. There is hardly anything edible here. Red and black skullberries are poisonous . If you eat just one of them, you will fall into a deep coma similar to death, from which you will not wake up again soon.

Norger forest

The spruces of this forest are hard as stone and their wood is black and stinking. Anyone trying to chop them down will need a sharp ax and patience. With every swing of the axe, the trees of the forest scream and shriek. This yelling will drive you insane.

Orcs and goblins and other disgusting figures love those screaming and lamenting. They process the wood into boxes, barrels and all sorts of useful things. Anything stored in barrels or boxes of this wood will go bad and inedible. This is precisely why this wood is so popular with orcs and goblins. Everything they eat becomes even more smelly and disgusting in such barrels. Just the way they like it best.

All sorts of malicious animals and nasty monsters crawl in the undergrowth. Wild stumps, slimy eyes, and dragon isopods are a few of these creatures. One should be particularly careful of spiders. Their sticky webs don't release anything,. They live together in larger families and fight over every morsel of meat. But if they are attacked, everyone sticks together like sisters and brothers would do. If you've just fought a nasty spider, you'll quickly find yourself facing a dozen.

Norger forest

All in all, the Norger Forest is an unfriendly and dangerous place. You should avoid it.

Where the Norger meets the Borger Forest, there seems to be an eternal battle between good and evil. Black spruce, slime mold, and poisonius fungi are trying to spread. Some oaks fall victim to them. But the Borger forest knows how to defend itself. Ferns, mosses, and oaks grow in the forest and drive away all evil. It's a constant back and forth. Sometimes one wins, sometimes the other.

The mines of Gorbar

High to the northeast lie the mountains of Gorbar. The Borger Forest grows on his slopes. The mountain dwarves have driven mines into the hard stone. Here they dig for metals, crystals, gems, gold, and silver.

Under the mountain, the dwarves have created huge caverns and halls in which they live. Everything you need to live can be found in these mines. They grow mosses, herbs, and mushrooms. In big underground lakes, they breed blindings (fish) and ox fish. Luminous mosses and tender-light grasses grow on the walls and ceilings. If you stroke these mosses and grasses, they start to glow. They then glow in a pleasant pale yellow light. Some halls are so brightly lit that you could think the morning sun is shining through the thick rocky walls.

In the mines, there are several hundred rooms, halls, caves, and caverns. There are large forges where the dwarves process their metals. The blacksmithing of the mountain dwarves has always been unsurpassed. Hammers, Axes, Shields, and Armor by Mountain Dwarfs are rare and very popular across Aros. Mountain dwarves like to keep them to themselves. They rarely trade weapons, armor, or shields. But they are happy to sell metals, crystals, gold, and silver for the right price to anyone effort it.

The mines of Gorbar

A wide forest road leads to the mines of Gorbar. Merchants travel here to shop and then sell those goods throughout Aros. The mines and the town of Versund are connected by a special relationship: they have always been active traders.

The entrance to the mines is secured by 7 heavy stone gates that can only be unlocked from the inside. Whenever a new king ascends the throne, the mine will be sealed for the next 100 years. All mountain dwarves then live in isolation from the outside world deep inside the mountain. This is how the new bond between the people and the king is to be tied and strengthened. But before the dwarves close the gates, they give a big party in front of the mine gates. Friends from all over Aros are invited to this 3-day feast. Elves, humans, shortlines, dwarves from other tribes, and even friendly orcs are invited to this big festival. After 3 days the mountain dwarves withdraw into their mine. After 100 years, the dwarves then joyfully emerge, a huge celebration commemorating the return to the active world of Aros.

The mines or Gorbar

Deep in the south of the Norger Forest Highland, in the Black Monutains, is an abandoned tunnel. The dwarves originally wanted to set up their mines there. The mountains here are full of minerals and treasures.

Orcs, goblins, and all kinds of monsters and evil fellows have attacked these tunnels again and again. Therefore these tunnels were abandoned. In legends and stories, however, it is said that there are still hidden treasures and weapons in these tunnels.

Gorb lach gelech
Mountain of Fire rivers

In the north of Aros lies Gorb lach gelech, the mountain of the rivers of fire. This mighty volcano rises high above the northern mountains of Aros. Its smoking peak is covered in snow most of the year. Like an overflowing beer mug, the hot lava flows down its sides into the valley. Numerous caves and entrances lead deep into the mountain.

A mighty labyrinth of branching paths and corridors runs through the whole mountain. Precious metals and glittering gems lie deep within. Many adventurers have lost their lives here. Hot lava streams, toxic gas clouds, and falling boulders make the journey through the volcano extremely difficult and dangerous. If that weren't bad enough, numerous fire monsters, isopods, and monsters live here. They are comfortable in the heat.

There are several hundred passages, caves, caverns, lava lakes, and rivers in Gorb lach gelech. Narrow stone bridges lead over deep lava canyons. Narrow corridors meander through the rock. Stalagmites growing out of the ground. Dripping lava causes to grow out of the rocky ground like jagged teeth.

Gorb lach gelech
Mountain of Fire rivers

Some caves are filled with large crystals of all colors. Many have delved for these riches; few have returned from the depths. Falling rocks, collapsing bridges, and rising lava flows block the path home for many. More than a few firelings and fire monsters have delighted in overwhelming the lost adventurer.

There is a narrow pass to Gorb lach gelech. This leads through the rocky northern mountains. This pass is snow-free in summer, but the first snowflakes fall here in early autumn. Snow makes crossing this pass nearly impossible.

Shieren Village and the Castle Loth

Almost in the center of Aros are the town of Shieren and the castle of Loth. Shieren was once a small village and the castle was just a small fortress. A long time ago, King Ralph the 1st reached the small, unassuming fortress. With a lot of love, foresight, and patience, he steadily expanded the fortress. With this expansion, Shieren also grew steadily. This is how Shieren became the largest town in Aros. The small fortress became a big castle.

In Shieren many people, elves, dwarves, orcs, and shortlines live peacefully together. Freedom and fraternity are the foundations of Shieren. Everyone is allowed to be who they are and live their way. That connects all residents of Shieren. Anyone who is from Shieren belongs to it, no matter what breed or class they come from. Strangers are always welcome in Shieren. However, anyone who does not abide by the laws of the fraternity will be severely punished in Shieren. No one is above the law of fraternity. No king, no governor, no cleric. All are to uphold the law of fraternity. The law states that everyone has the same rights and duties. Everyone must recognize the next one as a sister or brother. Anyone who sins against other citizens or groups has broken the law. For this reason, criminals and thieves are punished more severely here than in the rest of Aros.

Shieren Village and the Castle Loth

In Shieren there are a large number of dealers, institutions, craftsmen, doctors, and schools. There is a large library with a huge number of books on all subjects. There are nature, history, medicine, magic, and monster books as well as exciting adventure and fantasy novels. Everything a city need is available in Shieren. Education is very important here. That is why there are several schools and universities in Shieren. There is a nature and herbal school, a magic school with different branches, and a scientific academy that deals with plants, animals, and monsters in Aros. There is also the Academy of Dark Arts, but only a select few students are allowed to learn these magic arts.

Loth Castle stands in the center of Shieren. All buildings are in a circle around the castle. Shieren is protected by a large wall. There are 4 main gates. One in the north, east, south, and west. There is also a smaller entrance to the southwest. Here are the fields for grain, fruit, and vegetables. The farmers usually use this entrance after their work is done. The main gates close at 10 p.m. Anyone who still wants admission after that can do so at the smaller southwestern entrance or the main gate in the south. All others remain locked overnight.

Shieren Village and the Castle Loth

The natural healing and herbal school Frinda & Theerema in Shieren is the best known in the whole country. It was founded by Frinda and Theerema a few hundred summers ago. Frinda Bergsan was a mountain dwarf and nature lover from the mines of Gorbar. From an early age, she devoted herself to the medicinal plants in the Borger forest around the mines. For a long time, she was considered an oddball and an outsider among the dwarves. The mountain dwarves could not understand why she preferred to be in forests than underground. But she stayed true to her path and her heart.

Shierenvillage and the Castle Loth

Theerema Winterhair, daughter of the dwarf king Thonagund bush brow, at the age of only 19 summers suddenly fell seriously ill and her condition deteriorated so quickly that any outside help would come too late. By the time the news would reach the best healers in Aros, it would have been too late for her.

But Frida Bergsan knew what to do. So she saved Theerema's life with a carefully crafted decoction of herbs and medicinal plants. From that day on, there was an inseparable bond between the two. The bond was so strong that Theerema encouraged Frinda to found a school: an institution dedicated to herbal and naturopathic arts so that the whole realm of Aros could benefit from her knowledge. King Ralph ad only just begun work on the small fort when word of the school reached his ears. He immediately offered Frinda and Theerema his full support. about the project. He offered Frinda and Theerema his full support.

Since Shierenvillage was in the center of Aros, the two decided to set up their school there, much to thonagund's chagrin. His love for his daughter prompted him to send large sums of gold, metal, and craftsmen in order to finish the school quickly; his hope was that his beloved Theerema would return to his side soon after completion.

Shierenvillage and the Castle Loth

At this time, more mountain dwarves seem to live in Schieren than other citizens. With diligence and understanding, a wonderful school was created with spacious classrooms, gardens, and laboratories. Regular trips to the mines of Gorbar and the Borger Forest softened Thonagund sadness a bit. So he could see his daughter at least a few times of the year. When Thonagund suddenly died 10 summers later, Theerema knew that she had to accept her duty as the king's daughter. She took the throne and went into the mountain and sealed the great seven gates for the next 100 summers.

Frinda was the only mountain dwarf left outside the mine. After 100 summers had passed, Frinda and Theerema met again. Frinda had developed the school into a real institution. When Theerema visited Frinda in Schieren, her last days had already begun. She never really recovered from a serious accident. Frinda and Theerema spent the last few days together in Schieren. Frinda did not find her final resting place in Schieren, but in the Borger Forest above the mines of Gorbar, as she had wished at last. A statue of Frinda and Theerema still stands in the school's garden.

Shierenvillage and the Castle Loth

Every year, 250 students study here regularly, either full-time or part-time. In addition to sorcery, many young witches and wizards continue their education in natural medicine and herbs. There are classes for the use of gentle medicinal herbs and strong medicinal herbs, finding and recognizing medicinal herbs, herbal cultivation, making tinctures and potions, and natural medicine for dwarves, humans, elves, shortlings, orcs, animals, and monsters.

Shierenvillage and the Castle Loth

There are 2 larger and 2 smaller gardens where medicinal plants and herbs are cultivated. These gardens are always open and can be used by students 24 hours a day.

A few poisonous plants also grow in a small, enclosed garden. This garden can only accessible through the private quarters of the principal. There are 2 laboratories available to the students. Potions, juices, and tinctures can be produced and examined here.

Only the principal and caretakers live in the school. The current principal is Gald Rugenfedder, a gaunt older man with a balding head and long white hair down his sides. At first glance, he seems very serious and grim. But the impression is deceptive. Gald is a very funny and outgoing man. He has a deep and personal friendship with Gandolin from Versund. As a professional and Natural healer he is an absolute expert. There is no natural healer in all of Aros who knows more and can do more than he does. Many of the textbooks and illustrations used here come from Gandolin from Versund. For many years, Gald has tried to get Gandolin to move to Schieren. But Gandolin politely declined the request each time.

Shierenvillage and the Castle Loth

Schieren´s magic school is the largest in the country. Young witches and wizards learn their craft here. Like any school of magic, there are different classes and branches.

During the elementary school years, students learn the basics of sorcery and witchcraft. Simple spells are taught here as well as the proper use of the innate gift of sorcery. However, the elementary school does not mean that only smaller children are in these classes. Some people only discover their magic power later in life. The primary school classes are consistently mixed. All breeds and ages can be found here.

In the secondary classes, a distinction is made between branches. Not all wizards and witches are created equal, and some spells require more spell power than others. That doesn't mean that someone with less magic power is weaker than someone with more magic power. It just means they can't master that many different spells. A weaker caster who only specializes in 1 or 2 fire spells can perfect them, which can make them very powerful. The different branches of magic are healing spells, combat spells, conjuration, nature and weather spells, influence spells, and fortune (lucky) spells.

Shierenvillage and the Castle Loth

Around 650 students currently go to the magic school in Schieren. Attached to the school is a small boarding school where around 250 students and around 30 teachers live with their families on a regular basis. Most of the rooms in this boarding school are designed for 3-5 students. There is a large dining room and common areas for games or get-togethers.

The school itself has 28 classrooms including a spell room where summons can safely take place. Many spells and runes protect not only the students, but all of Aros from unspeakable dangers. A summoning spell gone wrong, however, can do a great amount of damage. they had spread around the school.

There is also an alchemy lab for potions and tinctures. The school receives the plants and herbs required for these potions from the natural healing and herbal school in Schieren.

Shierevillage and the Castle Loth

There is a battle room where spells for combat can be practiced and used safely. A classroom for nature and weather magic, affectionately called "The Forest" by the students, is a very large room housing many trees and plants that can be influenced by magic. The remaining rooms for study are quite spartan: a blackboard and school desks for up to 30 students.

The school has a library that includes almost 12,000 books and manuscripts from all over Aros on every aspect of magic. Many are old, ancient tomes that can only be read by well experienced mages. Within the library is a section under heavily protected lock and key: the most dangerous spellbooks in all Aros, books about the darkest, most evil, and/or most powerful magic, are kept here. Even a copy of Gandolin's most famous book, Magnal Gorgash, is kept here.

Shierenvillage and the Castle Loth

The Dark Arts Academy is right next to the magic school. Currently, the academy has only 3 students and 1 teacher. Songbeard Longhoof is the teacher of this academy. Along with Gandolin, he is the most powerful wizard in all of Aros. Songbeard is a strict but good-hearted Shortling. His enormous magic power allows him to control the dark arts without being seduced by them. Songbeard is the only person who has the key to the restricted section of the library. He knows each of the texts and has personally vouced for its inclusion in that section.

No one can access this knoweldge with Songbeard's approval. His tremendous magical prowess has helped not only Schierendorf, but all of Aros, many times. At the age of 14, a mere student at the Academy, Songbeard had to face a powerful wizard who had succumbed to the corruption of dark magic - his teacher, Grandhuf Blasage. In his tenure as an instructor, Grandhuf had gradually slipping into insanity and turned his back on all good. In a fight tto the death, Songbeard defeated his instructor; with his final breath, Grandhuf thanked Songbeard for freeing him from the darkness that consumed him. The trauma of that battle made it all to clear to Songbeard the severity of the dark magic, and he has never underestimated its power.

Shieren Village and the Castle Loth

Finally, there is the great hall, used as a meeting place for students. Once a month, a guest speaker comes to explain new spells, old unearthed customs, and any new and important rules relating to magic to the students. These events are renowned, and the halls is usually filled to capacity. Gandolin's performances are a real spectacle. In addition to great explanations and stories, there is a lot to laugh about; Gandolin is known throughout Aros as a master of jokes.

The scientific academy of Schierendorf deals with all manner of plant, animal, and monster within Aros. This academy is open to all citizens of Aros and is maintained by the king. In the front part, there is a natural history museum where patrons can admire varied and numerous preserved flora and fauna from all over Aros. The absolute highlight of the museum is a dragon skull from Fend al Nern, the dragon cemetery. In all, there are 45 scientists, scholars, and taxidermists working at the Academy of Natural Sciences. The leader is Rensai Goldswing, a tall elf from the realm of the golden elves. Adventurers, explorers, and researchers bring new animals, plants, and monsters to the Academy daily to be cataloged and researched. Many of these species are already know the the Academy scholars, but every one in a while, someone discovers something new.

Shierenvillage and the Castle Loth

Loth Castle sits on a small hill in the heart of Schieren. This once-small fortress has grown into a stately castle. Unfortunately, Aros currently has no real king. The son of the last king, Brinnfeld the Thin, was deposed for incompetence. Brinnfeld the Simple was not up to the office of the king, so he was summarily deposed by the people of Schieren. He lived in a small monastery near Versund until his death. His cousin Jamin Goodheart is currently in charge of the city. Jamin is a good thinker and leader. Despite his young age of only 28 summers, he is an exceedingly smart and kind-hearted leader.

Many in people petition for his election to the throne. In the castle, one looks in vain for superfluous splendor. The castle has always been designed to be functional and in accordance with the fraternal laws. Two large watchtowers are flanking the front of the castle. In the middle stands the main tower and the main gate. This gate can be reached via a stone bridge. In the inner courtyard is a building with a throne room, the living quarters of the current leader, and the kitchen. The guards live in the watchtowers. In addition to the pantry and armory, there are also smaller treasure chambers in the underground cellars. A secret passage leads into the well and from there through a narrow passage out of the castle. There is a smaller entrance on the right. This is secured 2 compartments and is used to delivering goods.

Shierenvillage and the Castle Loth

The main commercial road of the city winds through many alleys. Here you can buy almost everything your heart desires. Noble clothes are available here as well as weapons, armor and shields. All kinds of exotic food and drinks from all over Aros can be purchased here. Taverns and inns mix between the individual shops and stalls. A market with changing stalls takes place in the courtyard once a week. In addition to fruit and vegetables, special delicacies from all over Aros are also offered here.

The wasteland Amon Oman

In the south of Aros lies the desert of Aman Oman. Very few have ever crossed or cut through this desert. There seems to be nothing here but dust, rocks, and cacti. Large cactus groves grow on the edge of this desert. Many adventurers go to these groves to harvest cactus fruit to sell them, quite lucratively, in the markets of Schierenvillage.

Some cave entrances have recently been discovered at the edge of the cactus groves. A few corridors have been charted already and appear to be the start of a large labyrinthtine system of tunnels. These charts are maintained at the Natural Science Academy; those who are on good terms with the Academy's leader are welcome to see them.eader Rensai, can certainly see it.

In the middle of the desert rises the Great Red Mountain, Gorb Ren Amon. This peaked mountain is fringed with steep and jagged cliffs. None have dared to climb it. During the day, temperatures can rise well above 70 degrees, and it hasn't rained there for a very long time. Only adventurers who are bold and well-prepared (perhaps borderline foolish) would attempt to journey up the mountain.
Songs and legends of old tell of the Gorb Ren Amon. They tell of underground caves that hold entire cities deep within the rock. Whether these stories are true and whether the Amon people even exist have not been confirmed, even to this day.

Bunsbüchel

Bunsbüchel is a small farming village on the eastern slopes of the Dolgon Mountains. It lies high up between lush meadows and dense spruce forests. There are just 10 farmhouses and stables in Bunsbüchel. The people here live from what nature offers them and from the cheese and milk of their cows. Several dozen cows and their calves graze on the sunny pastures here in spring and summer. Numerous mountain streams and rivulets flow in narrow valleys and gorges. Narrow waterfalls flush the river in spring melting snow down into the valley.

Experienced and agile hikers need half a day to climb to Bunsbuchel. For slower, short-legged, or older hikers, the ascent can quickly take a whole day. The path starts quite flat but then begins sloping quite sharply. The way first leads through dense spruce forests which then become steadily more sparce. One must be wary of wolves and bears amongst the trees. About 2/3 of the way, there is a small stream to be crossed. Only a little water flows here typically, and most can cross by jumping from stone to stone. However, in spring or after heavy rainfall, this small stream can suddenly become a swift and raging river. The simple incovenience of crossing a tiny stream becomes a dangerous and daunting hazard to overcome; special care is best to be taken.

Bunsbüchel

There is a small inn with guest rooms in Bunsbüchel. Up to 6 travelers can stay here in 3 rooms. You can eat delicious homemade cheese, milk herb soup, roast mountain goats, and sweet rock chunks (Kaiserschmarn) with berry compote. The farmers make their way to Schierendorf twice a year to offer their homemade cheese for sale. Then only the children and old people stay behind.

If you follow the path behind the village, you get to the pass over the Dolgon Mountains. This pass was created long ago by the Golden elves to be able to traverse the mountains quickly. Since this pass is very dangerous, it is used extremely rarely.

Fen Galion

In the deciduous forests on the west side of the Dolgon Mountains lies the Golden Elf city of Fen Galion. Long ago, the golden elves built their city high in mighty chestnut trees. Green and gold are the colors of the gold elves of Fen Galion because a mighty vein of gold runs through the Dolgon. Because of this, for a long time, there were wars and disputes over the Dolgon. Both the dwarves and dragons and worms who love gold have long struggled for supremacy in the Dolgon. But the elves were always victorious.

The city cannot be seen from the outside. The chestnut trees of the elves blend in with the surrounding forests. Residential buildings, halls, and open spaces are located in the crowns of the trees. The branches of the trees intertwine in some places, forming bridges and steps. So all trees are connected. Curved carvings, ornaments, and archways adorn the habitat of the golden elves.

In the center of the city stands a mighty red chestnut tree; in its crown are the chambers of Furian Goldelb, the king of Fen Galion. He has ruled Fen Galion for several hundred years. He is known to be a kind, loving ruler. He keeps in close contact with other rulers and will try his best to quell hostile or quarreling parties. His queen is Sand Weisstraenne; as popular as Furian himself, she is a calm and levelheaded queen.

Galion Medin

Below Fen Galion lies the cave of Galion Medin.

The healing spring of the Dolgon is housed in this cave. The waters of this spring are known throughout Aros. It is said that a single drop has unmatched properties, healing most any injury in no time. In ancient times, a lot of water flowed from the spring which was fed by a large cistern within the mountain. Since an incident several decades ago, little water has been trickling from the spring, less and less water with each passing year.

Hopefully, many of the still unexplored corridors and paths deep within the mountain will be safely reached and charted.

Consta Paira

Consta Paira is a larger fishing nest on the west coast of Aros. In addition to fishermen and whalers, there are also a lot of shady characters romping about here. Nobody asks where you come from or what your name is. Many a crook has found his new home in Consta Paira.

3 large whalers and several small fishing boats are anchored in the harbor. Whalers are rough folk with strong arms and shut mouths. They only speak what is necessary and prefer to get things done rather than ramble on. Once a month they go out to sea to hunt for horn or plate whales. These huge monster fish are extremely aggressive and dangerous. Many whalers have already been torn from their boats and are now lying on the seabed. The killed whales are butchered, their meat cooked, and their horns or plates processed.

Consta Paira

In addition to the large whalers, there are numerous medium and small fishing boats. They use nets to hunt for glittery sailings, snow-capped deer, and black eels. These fish are processed and delivered to Schierendorf. The fish skin of black eels is used to make leather that is particularly light and tear-resistant. It is often worn under armor, providing mobility and additional protection.

Consta Paira has around 50 buildings. In addition to numerous smaller fishermen's houses, there is a large tavern with guest rooms, a tanner for fish leather, a whale butcher who butchers the animals, and the house of the mayor. The tavern called "The bickering Schmuhrenke" is a gloomy place. People smoke, drink, gamble, and fight here- not for the faint-hearted or cowardly. Anyone who comes here should avoid all eye contact and avoid making fun of the stench of fish This tavern is popularly known as "To the dentist" because anyone who fights here usually loses a few teeth. The narrow paths through the city all lead to the broad landscaped port. There are stalls selling fish, crabs, crabs, and other sea creatures.

Consta Paira

An old ship's doctor lives in a houseboat on one of the small offshore islands. Minhärd Gerenborn is a gaunt old but extremely friendly man. He practiced in Schierendorf for many years and was extremely popular there. His healing arts are known throughout the country. And now and then desperate patients make their way to Consta Paira to get his advice. Although Minhärd is very old, he still enjoys the best of health. Even in the middle of the night, he makes his way to patients if they need his help. His small but extremely comfortable houseboat is sheltered in a small bay.

Consta Paira

The mayor of Consta Paira is an unfriendly man named Font Bernsenker. It is rumored that he is actually the pirate Mor Herganson. One day, Mor disappeared, and a few days later, Font appeared in Consta Paira. No one knows for sure if the rumor is true, but there is one thing that keeps the rumor alive: Font bears a VERY strong resemblance to Mor Herganson.

As mayor, he leads Consta Paira with a strict, corrupt hand. Be that as it may, his leadership qualities cannot be denied, and he has saved the fishing nest from harm on multiple occasions. Nonetheless, he is a definite crook; his influence can be swayed with gold or anything else of value. Beneath his grumpy and rough exterior, however, lies a core of loyalty. His devotion to Consta Paira and its denizens is contrastingly noticeable.

Ruined City - Dahlon

Dahlon, in the southwest of Aros, was a small but mighty city many ages ago. In the many legends, one can read about the enormous wealth of the city. There are countless cellars, corridors, and caverns below the city that should still contain riches of gold, weapons, and magical artifacts. The city of Dahlon was founded by Honasch Liftnascher, a powerful wizard who, in his later years, ventured intensively in black and dark magic. Legend has it that Honasch once cast a spell so powerful that it not only reduced the city of Dahlon to rubble, but it spawned a massive horde of dark creatures. The zombies and undead emerged from the earth to attack the residents of Dahlon. With the last of his strength, Honasch created a protective circle around the city, ensuring that these terrible creatures can never leave Dahlon.

Many adventurers have dared to search for treasure in the ruins of Dahlon. Very few ever came back. Dahlon is a dangerous place, but it's still full of secrets and treasures. Honasch had a very large library of spell books and a Great Chamber full of spell artifacts. What more of that is useful, nobody knows.

Fend al Nern

The Fend al Nern Dragon Cemetery is a mysterious and spooky place. Nobody knows what happened here long ago. Dragon skeletons, bones, and skulls are strewn throughout Fend al Nern.

Between countless dragon skeletons, there are indications of a magical fight between dragons, magicians, and unknown beings. Who was on the good side here? Who were the bad guys in this fight? No one in all of Aros knows exactly what happened here.

Berghof Brandlöscher, a shortling, has devoted himself to the dragon cemetery of Fend al Nern since his youth. Nobody has studied this place more intensively than he. For more than 60 years he has been collecting clues, bones, and artifacts to solve this mystery once and for all.

Fend al Nern does not give away its secrets lightly. This vast plain with its rolling hills looks idyllic at first glance. Upon closer inspection, one quickly realizes that the scattered rocks are not made of stone. These are bones Hundreds, maybe even thousands of bones are scattered here. Some are as big as entire houses.

A family of four could live in some skulls, each with its room.

Plants and Fungi

A variety of plants and mushrooms grow in Aros. Many are very useful or particularly tasty. Plants can heal, give light, or if not careful, bring death.

Whoever roams through the forests of Aros will surely discover some unknown plants. If you want to know more about plants, you can get information in the Natural Science Museum of Aros.

(The big book of plants and mushrooms from Aros will be published in 2023)

Plants and Fungi

luminous moss

This moss likes to grow in dark and damp places. It is often found on the walls and ceilings of cellars or caves. Luminous moss glows faintly. If you rub it between your hands, it starts to glow brightly and is ideal as a torch. The luminosity lasts about 1 hour. After that it only glows faintly. Luminous moss is completely non-toxic, but is still not suitable for consumption. It tastes very bitter and can trigger diarrhea.

Red snotty boletus (mushroom)

The red snotty boletus is related to the slime mold. This red funnel-shaped mushroom spits or drools reddish mucus. Insects get trapped in this slime, which the fungus then slowly digests. The slime of the boletus is excellent as an adhesive. It is edible but has a very distinctive taste. It tastes like warm snot, which makes it unpopular in Aros kitchens.

Green throat cracker

This green umbrella mushroom not only looks delicious, it is too. The throat cracker is a very tasty mushroom that tastes delicious when cooked. Its pepper note makes it extremely popular. But be careful, the throat cracker is sharp. The young mushrooms are only slightly hot, but the older and larger the mushrooms get, the hotter they become. Adult throat crackers can reach a height of 30 cm. These adult mushrooms are very, very hot. Even the strongest orcs and dwarves are knocked out by such a mushroom. It got his name from Singrood Moosschelte. He is the only one who has ever eaten a bite from an adult throat cracker. He was a wood elf from Fen Galion. Singrood outwitted the dragon Gef Chaldorn in an eating contest. The dragon gasped and could no longer breathe fire. This is how Singrood got away from Moss Scold. But this story should be told elsewhere. Since then, the mushroom has been called the throat cracker.

Giant berries

Giant berries are not uncommon in Aros. There are giant blueberries, gooseberries, raspberries, blackberries and strawberries. Giant berries can grow as big as an orc's head and are extremely tasty. 2 large berries can be enough to feed a hungry dwarf, or at least to satiate them in the short term. But all kinds of monsters also like to cavort in such fields and bushes. So be careful when picking, always keep your eyes and ears open.

White star thorn (healing)

The white star thorn: a green plant with large white blooming petals that have healing properties. The leaves can be chewed into a paste and placed on a wound or brewed into a very powerful medicinal tea. White star thorn is very rare. It prefers to grow in light deciduous forests between ferns and large grasses; the star thorn has also been discovered in dark, damp spruce forests. Some have even been found in caves. In these environments, the plants grow much smaller, limiting their healing potential. When chewed, the star thorn can restore up to 5 health from external wounds. A quickly prepared tea can regenerate up to 8 points of health. However, cooking a broth for 8 hours can offer up to 15 health points, restoring 2 health per hour of cooking.

Fangfern

Also known as catch fern, this slightly blue fern likes to grow in the bright spots or along the edges of forests. The catch fern is so named because it grabs at its prey. Whatever gets too close to the large leaves can become ensnared in a strong grasp. That makes the fern particularly suitable for the production of naturally sturdy ropes or bowstrings. The stalks of the mature leaves can be crushed between stones, separating the individual fibers for further processing. Be warned - large fields of fangfern can engulf a full-sized human, dwarf, or orc, keeping them permanently in one place. Many adventurers have met their end in a field of fangfern..

Eyelings and Blindlings (healing)

These umbrella mushrooms look confusingly similar. But their effects are completely different. The blindling is slightly darker on the underside of the top than the eyeling. Anyone who eats a blindling can no longer see for several hours, sometimes even days. The only known antidote is the eyeling. Anyone who eats such a mushroom immediately regains their vision. Eyelings can heal any form of non-permanent blindness. The eyeling also heals blindness caused by poison or magic. Whoever finds these mushrooms must make an Intelligence +2 test to be able to distinguish between the mushrooms with certainty. Whoever is eats the mushroom anyway must pass an staminia skill check+3. A failed check means it was a a blindling.

velvet wave

The Velvet Wave is a black mushroom that grows in long curving forms on the forest floor. It looks like a gathered fabric border. The velvet wave is the most poisonous mushroom in all of Aros and is extremely rare. If you find one, you should never touch it with your bare skin. Their venom can enter the body through the pores and kill you. To this day, there is no known antidote for poisons brewed from velvet waves. Since velvet waves are so extremely rare, the natural science academy in Schierendorf pays handsome prices for them. Velvet waves are best left in glasses or barrels for transport.

Phoenix feather (healing)

"Anyone who hasn't been dead for long, can brought back and was never gone." The Phoenix Feather brings adventurers who have just died back to life. Nobody knows yet whether the phoenix feather is a feather of a real phoenix or just a wild plant. A real phoenix has never been seen in Aros. In the natural science academy of Schierendorf for decades there has been a dispute if it is a feather or a plant. This feather is placed on the chest of the newly deceased, whereupon the heart begins to beat again and they wakes up fully recovered from his slumber. Phoenix feathers are very rare in Aros. Whoever finds one should take good care of it or sell it to the highest bidder.

Red Bob berry

Love spells are not often found, but if one is to be prepared then the red bob berry is essential. This small, round berry resembles a bottom: the two halves of the berry meet with a seam down the middle. It isn't poisonous, but it isn't tasty either. When brewed, however, the full potential of the berry is unleashed. This concoction is known as a love spell. With only a few drops put into a drink, a strong sense of attraction overcomes the drinker. The one who carries the potion container becomes the object of affection. One must be sure to be careful lest the bottle fall into the hands of a crafty and opportunistic creature. Or the enchanted one might find themselves with a monster of a crush.

Money in Aros

In Aros, there is much that can be bought and sold. Trading and bartering are more than common occurances, it is the expected method of commerce. Coins called shillings are the official currency of Aros.

The smallest unit is the bronze shilling (1€).
10 bronze shillings are worth 1 silver shilling (€10).
10 silver shillings are worth 1 gold shilling (€100).

You can give heroes between 20 and 50 bronze shillings as starting credit.

Prices:
Drinks in taverns and pubs - 1 bronze shilling
large lunch or dinner - 2 bronze shillings
Overnight stay in an inn - 4-5 bronze shillings
3 apples - 1 bronze shilling
1/2 kg carrots - 1 bronze shilling
big fish - 1 bronze shilling
Loaf of Bread - 1 bronze shilling

Money in Aros

Weapons:

a small simple dagger - 8 bronze shillings

a small simple short sword - 14 bronze shillings

a plain bow - 10 bronze shillings

a simple helmet - 10 bronze shillings

a plain shield - 11-14 bronze shillings

a simple battle-axe - 12 bronze shillings

a simple throwing ax - 15 bronze shillings

a simple armor - 20 bronze shillings

Backpack - 3 bronze shillings

a simple crossbow - 16 bronze shillings

10 arrows - 4 bronze shillings

a shirt made of Schmurenken leather - 13 bronze shillings

a simple horse - 20 bronze shillings

game board

Adventures in Aros is designed to be a classic pen and paper RPG. You can play with or without a board. Game boards are mostly used to better represent combat or complex game scenarios. Battles can be executed more tactically.

Most game boards are grid-based with 1" squares. Adventures in Aros has a game board, books, and a system of 3D printable assets that can be used.

game board

Combat is easier to represent visually using a board. Battles can be done tactically. A fight that would be played out within the imagination of the players can now been seen in-person. Like a game of chess, heroes and monsters can now move around the board.

Fight stats

Skills

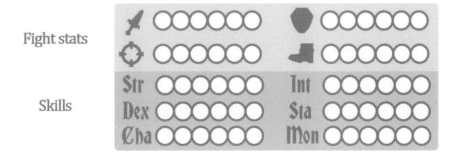

Combat values can be transferred directly to the game board. Range ⊕ and movement ◢ values are measured in squares on the game board.
A range of 3 means 3 squares of movement on the board.
A move of 4 means the player can move 4 squares on the board.

Movement

How far a hero can move is symbolized by the 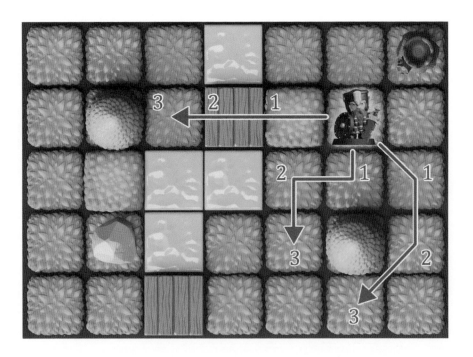 shoe. In each round of combat, the player can move according to the value. The player can move straight, sideways and diagonally.

Changes of direction within a turn are allowed. Trees, monsters and other obstacles cannot be jumped over. Shallow water can be walked through. There is an stamina skill check on swimming.

range

A hero's or monster's attack range  is shown by the range icon. The hero can reach this range with his weapon. So a bow usually has a larger reach than a knife. The field on which the opponent is standing is always counted. With a range of 3, the player has 2 free squares between himself and the opponent.

There are 2 systems used to determine attack range.

direct system
vision system

The **direct system** is simpler and more suitable for children and beginners. In the direct system, a straight or diagonal line must be able to be drawn from the player to the opponent. This line always runs through the center of all crossed squares.

With the **vision system**, the enemy must be in sight, but not in direct range. The opponent can be within range without being able to draw a direct straight line to the opponent.

direct system

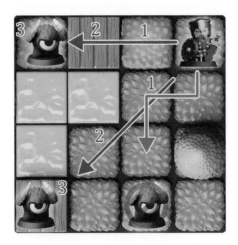

Here you can see 3 enemies in sight, but only 2 of them can be hit. The monster with the blue arrow is in the player's field of vision, but you cannot draw a straight line across the center of the squares to the monster.

The player cannot attack the monster and the monster cannot attack the player. This variant is simpler than the vision system. Players just need to pay attention to direct lines. If an opponent isn't in a straight or diagonal line to the player, they don't pose a threat. This is easier to grasp, especially for children.

sight system

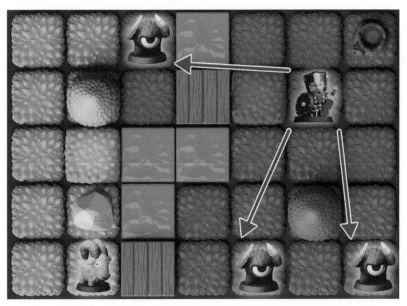

The player has all 4 monsters in view. He can draw a straight line from a corner of his square to any corner of the opponent's square. Even if the line does not go directly through the center of other fields. However, the field must be within the weapon's range. The mountain goat is out of range of 3. It can't be reached within 3 fields.

This variant is more realistic and offers more flexibility. However, it is more difficult to constantly keep an eye on all opponents and their range. Therefore, this variant is not optimal for children and beginners.

game board

Any 1" or 25mm grid-based game board can be used.

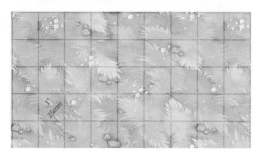

Azargames currently offers a modular 3D printable system for the Adventures of Aros. This system can be set up and rebuilt as you like, and gameboard-books are also available on which the 3D-printed elements can be placed.

On www.Myminifactory.com/Florian Azar and www.azar-games.de you will find all currently available products.

Gallery

With the Azarbricks system, you can create a small, medium, large and even very large sets. Here are a few examples of what you can do with it.

Gallery

Printed in Great Britain
by Amazon